"You find me attractive?"

"Yes," Sin-Jin shouted again, then lowered his voice, "in a very irritating sort of way." He took the empty glass out of her hand and put it squarely on the table. "Now, I think it's time you showed me where this car of yours allegedly died."

Sherry looked up with wide eyes. "I don't think I can do that."

"And why is that?"

Spacious or not, the room began to feel as if it closed in on her and there was this awful pain emanating from the center of her body. "Because I think my water just broke."

Sin-Jin was almost disappointed. You'd really think a reporter could do better than that. "Ms. Campbell, I wasn't born yesterday or the day before that."

She was having trouble breathing. "I don't think that when you were born is going to be an issue, but this baby…wants to be born…today."

Dear Reader,

Make way for spring—as well as some room on your reading table for six new Special Edition novels! Our selection for this month's READERS' RING—Special Edition's very own book club—is *Playing by the Rules* by Beverly Bird. In this innovative, edgy romance, a single mom who is sick and tired of the singles scene makes a deal with a handsome divorced hero—that their relationship will not lead to commitment. But both hero and heroine soon find themselves breaking all those pesky rules and falling head over heels for each other!

Gina Wilkins delights her readers with *The Family Plan*, in which two ambitious lawyers find unexpected love—and a newfound family—with the help of a young orphaned girl. Reader favorite Nikki Benjamin delivers a poignant reunion romance, *Loving Leah*, about a compassionate nanny who restores hope to an embittered single dad and his fragile young daughter.

In *Call of the West*, the last in Myrna Temte's HEARTS OF WYOMING miniseries, a celebrity writer goes to Wyoming and finds the ranch—and the man—with whom she'd like to spend her life. Now she has to convince the cowboy to give up his ranch—and his heart! In her new cross-line miniseries, THE MOM SQUAD, Marie Ferrarella debuts with *A Billionaire and a Baby*. Here, a scoop-hungry—and pregnant—reporter goes after a reclusive corporate raider, only to go into labor just as she's about to get the dirt! Ann Roth tickles our fancy with *Reforming Cole*, a sexy and emotional tale about a willful heroine who starts a "men's etiquette" school so that the macho opposite sex can learn how best to treat a lady. Against her better judgment, the teacher falls for the gorgeous bad boy of the class!

I hope you enjoy this month's lineup and come back for another month of moving stories about life, love and family!

Best,

Karen Taylor Richman
Senior Editor

A Billionaire and a Baby

MARIE FERRARELLA

Silhouette®
SPECIAL EDITION™
Published by Silhouette Books
America's Publisher of Contemporary Romance

To Brenda and Frank Corl,
with affection.

SILHOUETTE BOOKS

ISBN 0-373-24528-9

A BILLIONAIRE AND A BABY

This edition published by arrangement with Harlequin Books S.A.

Visit Silhouette at www.eHarlequin.com

Printed in U.S.A.

Books by Marie Ferrarella in Miniseries

ChildFinders, Inc.
A Hero for All Seasons IM #932
A Forever Kind of Hero IM #943
Hero in the Nick of Time IM #956
Hero for Hire IM #1042
An Uncommon Hero Silhouette Books
A Hero in Her Eyes IM #1059
Heart of a Hero IM #1105

Baby's Choice
Caution: Baby Ahead SR #1007
Mother on the Wing SR #1026
Baby Times Two SR #1037

Baby of the Month Club
Baby's First Christmas SE #997
Happy New Year—Baby! IM #686
The 7lb., 2oz. Valentine Yours Truly
Husband: Optional SD #988
Do You Take This Child? SR #1145
Detective Dad World's Most Eligible Bachelors
The Once and Future Father IM #1017
In the Family Way Silhouette Books
Baby Talk Silhouette Books
An Abundance of Babies SE #1422

Like Mother, Like Daughter
One Plus One Makes Marriage SR #1328
Never Too Late for Love SR #1351

The Bachelors of Blair Memorial
In Graywolf's Hands IM #1155
M.D. Most Wanted IM #1167
Mac's Bedside Manner SE #1492
Undercover M.D. IM #1191

Two Halves of a Whole
The Baby Came C.O.D. SR #1264
Desperately Seeking Twin Yours Truly

Those Sinclairs
Holding Out for a Hero IM #496
Heroes Great and Small IM #501
Christmas Every Day IM #538
Caitlin's Guardian Angel IM #661

The Cutlers of the Shady Lady Ranch
(Yours Truly titles)
Fiona and the Sexy Stranger
Cowboys Are for Loving
Will and the Headstrong Female
The Law and Ginny Marlow
A Match for Morgan
A Triple Threat to Bachelorhood SR #1564

***The Reeds**
Callaghan's Way IM #601
Serena McKee's Back in Town IM #808

***McClellans & Marinos**
Man Trouble SR #815
The Taming of the Teen SR #839
Babies on His Mind SR #920
The Baby Beneath the Mistletoe SR #1408

***The Alaskans**
Wife in the Mail SE #1217
Stand-In Mom SE #1294
Found: His Perfect Wife SE #1310
The M.D. Meets His Match SE #1401
Lily and the Lawman SE #1467

***The Pendletons**
Baby in the Middle SE #892
Husband: Some Assembly Required SE #931

The Mom Squad
A Billionaire and a Baby SE #1528

*Unflashed series

MARIE FERRARELLA

earned a master's degree in Shakespearean comedy and, perhaps as a result, her writing is distinguished by humor and natural dialogue. This RITA® Award-winning author's goal is to entertain and to make people laugh and feel good. She has written over one hundred books for Silhouette, some under the name Marie Nicole. Her romances are beloved by fans worldwide and have been translated into Spanish, Italian, German, Russian, Polish, Japanese and Korean.

Come join the fun and excitement of Marie Ferrarella's new miniseries, *The Mom Squad*—four single mothers who come together to experience life's greatest miracle.

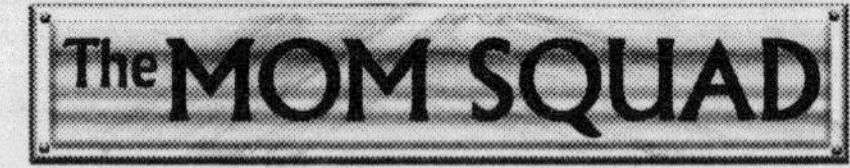

is...

Sherry Campbell—newswoman extraordinaire, benched when her boss discovered her little predicament....
A Billionaire and a Baby, SE #1528, available March 2003

Joanna Prescott—this teacher wanted a baby more than anything, and she found one at the local sperm bank!
A Bachelor and a Baby, SD #1503, available April 2003

Chris "C.J." Jones—as an FBI agent and expectant mother, C.J. was always on the go, even when the risks were high. Was love and happily-ever-after just what C.J.'s heart needed?
The Baby Mission, IM #1220, available May 2003

Lori O'Neill—at the helm, this Lamaze teacher soothed and instructed her pregnant charges—and had her own little bundle about to appear.
Beauty and the Baby, SR#1668, available June 2003

Chapter One

"Don't I know you from somewhere?"

The question was finally directed at Sherry Campbell after ten minutes of covert and not-so-covert staring on the part of the new office assistant as she copied a file. The assistant, standing at the *Bedford World News*'s centrally located copy machine, wasn't even aware that the state-of-the-art machine had ceased to spit out pages and was now content to sit on its laurels, waiting for her next move.

The assistant's next move, apparently, was to continue staring. Her brow furrowed as she attempted to concentrate and remember just where and when she had seen her before.

Sherry stifled a sigh of annoyance.

It wasn't that she was unaccustomed to that look of vague recognition on a person's face. Sometimes

Sherry was successfully "placed," but as time went on, not so often. There was a time, at the height of her previous career, where that was a regular occurrence. She couldn't say that she really minded. Then.

These days, however, people were just as apt to rudely stare at her swollen belly as they were at her face, that being the reason why her former career was a thing of the past. It was her unscheduled pregnancy that had gotten her dismissed from her anchor job and brought her to this junction in her life. Not in so many words, of course. Television studios and the people who ran them had an almost pathological fear of being sued because of some PC transgression on their parts. So when she had begun to show and told Ryan Matthews of her pregnancy, the executive producer of the nightly news had conveniently found a way to slip her into something less visible than the five o'clock news anchor position.

Within a day of her notifying Matthews that her waistline was going to be expanding, he had given her place to newcomer Lisa Willows and transformed her into senior copy editor, whimsically calling the move a lateral one. When she'd confronted him with his transparent motives, he'd lamely told her that demographics, even in this day and age, wouldn't have supported her "flaunting her free lifestyle." People, he'd said, still found unmarried pregnant women offensive and weren't about to welcome them into their living rooms night after night.

Matthews's words, even after five months, still rang in her ears. The fact that Sherry delivered the news behind a desk that was more than equal to hiding her increasing bulk from the general public, and that she'd never had a so-called free lifestyle—the pregnancy having arisen from her one and only liaison, a man who took no responsibility other than giving her the name of an abortion clinic—carried no weight with Matthews. With his spine the consistency of overcooked spaghetti, Matthews bent in the general direction of the greatest pressure. In this case it was the studio heads.

"If they can shoot around pregnant actresses on sitcoms to hide their conditions, why not me?" Sherry had insisted, but even then she knew it was no use. Matthews's mind had been made up for him. She was politely and firmly offered her new position or the door.

She took the door.

Her first inclination to "sue the pants off the bastard" faded, even as her friends and family rallied around her, echoing the sentiment. The last thing Sherry wanted was to draw negative attention to the baby she was carrying. She'd come to the conclusion that the less attention, the better.

In mulling over her options, she'd decided to take her circumstance as a sign that she should return to her first love: the written word. This meant following in her father's footsteps. Connor Campbell had been a well-respected, Pulitzer Prize–winning journalist before his retirement. It was because of him that she had gone into the news business in the first place.

Determination had always been her hallmark. So, after allowing herself an afternoon to grieve over her late, lamented career, Sherry moved full steam ahead, firing all torpedoes. She went to Owen Carmichael, her father's best friend and her godfather and asked for a job. Having started out with her father in the days before electric typewriters, Owen Carmichael was now the editor in chief of the *Bedford World News.*

Owen had been glad to hire her. Of course, she'd thought that he'd start her out with something a little more meaty than lighter-than-air fluff.

That was where her mind was right now, on the latest puff piece she was facing, not the assistant who stared at her with intense blue eyes and a puzzled frown on her face.

Sherry didn't feel like going into her previous life, or the reasons for the change. She felt too irritable for anything beyond a polite dismissal. Also the woman had the look about her that said she lived to gossip.

"I get that a lot," she told the other woman cavalierly. "I've got one of those faces people think they've seen before."

The assistant looked unconvinced. "But—" And then the woman paused, thinking. Suddenly, her whole face lit up as if a ray of inspiration had descended on her. "Say 'Hello, from the L.A. Basin.'"

That was her catchphrase, certainly nothing profound, but different enough to be remembered upon daily repetition. And she had been nightly anchor for four years before Matthews has ushered her out the door.

Sherry shook her head, her light-auburn hair swaying like a velvety wave about her oval face. "Sorry, I have to get upstairs to see Owen. Posthaste." She made it sound as if Owen was sending for her rather than the other way around. She was preparing to beard the lion in his den. Glancing at the dormant copy machine, Sherry pointed at it. "I think it needs feeding."

With that she hurried off, aware that the woman was still staring after her.

Hurrying these days was no small accomplishment for Sherry. She felt as if she was carrying around a lead weight strapped to her midsection. A lead weight that felt as if it was in constant flux.

On her way to the elevators, she tried not to wince as she felt another kick land against her ribs. At this rate she was going to need internal reconstructive surgery once her little squatter moved out.

"Don't you ever sleep?" she muttered to her stomach. She'd dragged herself into the office this morning because she'd been up half the night. Little whosit-whatsit was apparently learning the rumba. Either that or the baby had found a way to smuggle a motorcycle in there and had entertained itself through the wee hours of the night by constantly revving it up.

She'd been in no mood for what she found on her desk when she'd arrived. This week's assignment was even worse than last week's and she'd been convinced that that was the pits.

Breezing past Rhonda, her godfather's secretary, a woman whose curves detracted from the fact that she had a razor-sharp mind and practically ran the department in Owen's absence, Sherry walked straight into the managing editor's office.

"Owen," Sherry announced with more drama than she'd intended, "we have to talk. Please," she tagged on. As a further afterthought, she closed the door behind her.

Owen Carmichael barely glanced up from his computer. Mind-numbing statistics and figures were spread across the screen, bearing testimony to various polls conducted by the paper's PR department. He was scanning the figures while on his feet, his hands planted on the desk, his body leaning forward at an uncomfortable angle. It was an idiosyncrasy of his. He claimed he thought better in this position.

Of average height and far-less-than-average weight, he wore a shirt that was almost the same light color as his pants. With his semibald head, Owen gave the impression of an oversize Q-tip that someone had been nervously plucking at.

He glanced in his goddaughter's direction with almost no recognition. His mind was clearly somewhere other than in the room.

''Not now, Sherry.''

She'd known the man as long as she'd known her own parents and was just as at ease with him as with them. Others might cower when he took on that low tone, but Sherry wasn't among them.

''Yes, now.'' She plunked the assignment on his desk, feeling that it spoke for itself. ''It's not that I'm not grateful for the job, Owen,'' she began.

He raised his eyes to her face before lowering them back to the screen. ''Then do it.''

All right, maybe the assignment wasn't speaking, maybe it was whispering. She moved the sheet closer to him on the desk until the edge of the page touched one of his spread-out fingers. ''Just what the hell is this?''

He spared it a glance. The title jumped out at him. "An assignment."

"No," Sherry corrected slowly, her voice deceptively low. "It's a fluff piece." By now she'd thought she would have graduated out of that classification, moved on to something with teeth, or muscle or an iota of substance. Her voice rose an octave as frustration invaded it. "It's less than fluff. If I wasn't holding it down, it would float away in the breeze, it's that lightweight."

Owen sighed, looking up from the computer in earnest now. "There're no breezes in the office—other than the ones generated by overenergetic junior journalists flapping their lips. Aren't women in your condition supposed to be tired all the time, Sherry? Why aren't you tired?"

He didn't know the half of it, but she felt this need to prove herself, to lay the groundwork for a stellar career. Her parents had raised her not to do anything by half measures.

Loving Drew fell under that category. Had she not leaped in with both feet, she would have realized that he wasn't the type to stick around once the going got the slightest bit difficult.

"I am tired," she told Owen, doing her best not to sound it. "Tired of standing on the sidelines, tired of doing pieces people line their birdcages with."

One painfully thin shoulder rose and fell with careless regard. "Then write them snappier and they'll read them before lining the birdcage."

She wasn't in the mood for his humor. "Owen, I'm a serious journalist."

"And I'm a serious managing editor." He temporarily abandoned his search and looked at her. ''Right now there's no place I can put you but in this department. The first opening that comes up for an investigative reporter, I promise you'll have first crack at it. But right now, Sherry, I need you to be a good scout and—''

She didn't want to hear it. Sherry splayed her hands on his desk, carefully avoiding the almost stereotypically grungy coffee mug filled with cold black liquid. ''Owen, please. Something to sink my teeth into, that's all I ask. Something more challenging than searching for a new angle on the latest local school's annual jog-a-thon and/or bake sale.'' Sherry leaned over the desk, her blue eyes pleading with his. ''Please.''

''So, you think you're up to a challenge?''

''Yes, oh, yes,'' she cried with enthusiasm. ''An exposé, something undercover. I'm perfect for it.'' Straightening, she waved both hands over her far-from-hidden bulk. ''Who'd suspect a pregnant woman?''

''All right, you want a challenge, you got a challenge.''

Opening up the side desk drawer that the people who worked with him laughingly referred to as no-man's-land, Owen took out a canary-yellow file folder and handed it to her.

Sherry took the folder from him, noting that it felt as if it hardly weighed anything. Opening it, she discovered that there was a reason for that. It was empty.

''What am I supposed to do with this?'' She raised a brow, waiting.

"Fill it," he told her mildly.

Pregnancy had all but eradicated her normally ample supply of patience. It was difficult to keep emotion out of her voice. "With what?"

"With a story on St. John Adair."

Second verse, same as the first, she thought. This wasn't what she'd been talking about. "But—"

Knowing what was coming, Owen cut her off. "Not just a story, a biography." For emphasis, he spread his bony hands out in the air, as if touching the pages of a phantom newspaper. "I want everything you can find on this man. More."

And here, just for a moment, she'd thought he was being serious. Instead, he was asking for one of those simpering write-ups in the People section. Frustration threatened to cut off her air supply. She tossed the folder on his desk in disgust. "Owen, this is just a dressed-up fluff piece on steroids."

"Oh, really?" He picked up the folder. "St. John Adair, raider par excellence of the corporate world, the mere mention of whose name sends CEOs dashing off the sunny golf course and to their medicine cabinets in search of the latest high-tech antacids. The man who's fondly referred to as Darth Vader by even his closer associates. The man who has no biography, is said to have arrived on the scene full-grown, springing out of some shaking multi-mega business corporation's worst nightmare."

She was aware of the man's name, but not his awesome power. The focus of her interests lay elsewhere. "Business corporations don't have nightmares."

Owen's thin lips curved. "They have Adair," he

contradicted. "And we have nothing on him. No one does." He held out the folder to her. "You want a challenge, there's your challenge. Find out everything you can on Adair—find out more than everything you can on him," he amended. "I want to know what elementary school he went to, what his parents' names are, does he even have parents or was he suckled by wolves in the Los Angeles National Forest like Pecos Bill—"

Sherry struggled to keep back a smile. This was way over the top, but she had to admit, Owen had her curious. "Pecos Bill didn't grow up in the Los Angeles National Forest—"

"Good, that's a start." He tendered the folder to her again. "Give me more."

Eyeing him, she took the folder from Owen. "You're serious."

"Yes, I'm serious. Nobody else has managed to get anything on him or out of him other than 'Veni, vidi, vici.' I came, I saw, I conquered."

"I don't need the translation, Owen. Julius Caesar, talking about his triumphs," she added in case he was going to clarify that for her, as well.

Owen had launched into his coaxing mode, one of the attributes that made him good at his job. "You can be the first on your block to find something out on him." He pretended to peer at her. "Unless, of course, you think it's too hard—" He reached for the folder.

It was a game. She knew what he was up to and because of the friendship that existed between them, played along. She backed away to keep him from reaching the folder. "No, it's not too hard."

The grin transformed what could charitably be called a homely face into an amazingly pleasant one. "That's my girl."

She looked at the folder, already planning strategy. "When's the deadline?"

"The sooner the better. You tell me."

Now that she thought of it, she remembered her father saying something about Adair. Something along the lines of his coming out of nowhere and creating quite a sensation. Her first impulse was to call her father and ask if he had any connections that could lead her to the man, but she quickly squelched that. She wasn't about to walk a mile in borrowed shoes unless there was no other way. She didn't want to be her father's daughter, she wanted to be Sherry Campbell, use her own devices, her own sources.

She turned the folder around in her hand. "And you really think of this as an investigative piece?"

Owen gave her his most innocent expression. "Is this the face of a man who'd lie to you?"

She couldn't help but laugh. "As I recall, you're the one who told me about the Tooth Fairy."

To that, he could only plead self-defense. "Your tooth had fallen out. You were crying your eyes out." He spread his hands out. "You were five years old. What was I supposed to do?"

"Exactly what you did." Wheels began to spin. Mentally she was already out of the office. Sherry slapped her hand across the folder, her eyes sparkling. "Okay, you're on."

"Great." He was already back looking at the computer screen. "Don't forget to shut the door on your way out." The assignment she'd brought in was still on his desk. He held it up. "And give this other piece to Daly."

She darted back to retrieve the paper. "I'll do it in my spare time."

He nodded, satisfied. "Good." The familiar sound he was waiting for didn't register. Owen glanced up from his screen. "The door?"

Sherry nodded as she crossed the threshold and eased the door closed behind her.

A smile sprouted and took root as she deposited the assignment into the yellow folder and tucked it under her arm. It wasn't the kind of thing she'd been after, but if it was a challenge, then she was more than up to it. God knew she needed something meaty to work on before she completely lost her mind.

The woman's voice, crisp, clear, with "no nonsense" written over every syllable, echoed in Sherry's ear, "No, I am afraid that Mr. Adair is much too busy to see you. Try again next month. At the moment he's booked solid."

The woman sounded as if she was about to hang up. "The man has to eat sometime," Sherry interjected quickly, hoping for a break. "Maybe I could meet with him then."

She could almost hear the woman sniff before saying, "Mr. Adair has only working lunches and dinners. As I've already said—"

Undaunted, Sherry jumped back in the game. "Breakfast, then. Please, just a few minutes." That was all she needed for openers, she thought, but there was no reason to tell the guardian at the gate that.

Unmoved, the woman replied, "I'm sorry, I can't help you."

"But—"

The next moment Sherry found herself talking to a dial tone.

With a sigh she hung up. She was getting lazy, she thought. The way to get somewhere was in person, not over the telephone. She knew that. If the mountain wouldn't come to Mohammed, then Mohammed damn well was going to come to the mountain. With climbing gear.

Although these days, she thought, pushing herself up out of her chair, she wasn't sure just which part she would be cast in, Mohammed or the mountain.

The meeting had run over. It was within his power to call an end to it at any time, but Sin-Jin Adair liked to choose his moments. Authority wasn't something he believed in throwing around like a Frisbee; it was a weapon, to be used wisely, effectively. So he had sat and listened to the employees that he'd culled over the past few years, as he'd taken over one corporation after another. Keep the best, discard the rest. It was a motto he lived by.

A bastardization of his father's edict. Except that his father had applied it to women. Sin-Jin never did.

"Leaving early, I see."

He nodded at his secretary. Like everyone else around her, Edna Farley was the soul of efficiency. He and Edna had a history together, and her loyalty was utterly unshakable. It was another quality he demanded, but one he could be patient about. He valued the kind that evolved naturally, not one that was bought and paid for. If you could buy loyalty easily, then it could just as easily be sold to a higher bidder, thereby rendering it useless. That he paid his people top dollar ensured that they would not be tempted to look elsewhere in search of worldly goods.

"Not as early as I'd like. Go home, Mrs. Farley."

"Yes, sir." The woman peered out into the hall as he strode out. "Don't forget the Cavannaugh meeting tomorrow. And Mr. Renfro said he would be calling you at eight tomorrow morning."

"Good night, Mrs. Farley."

Walking away, he smiled to himself as the less-than-dulcet tones of Mrs. Farley echoed behind him, reminding him of appointments he didn't need to be reminded of. Everything he needed to know about his schedule was not tucked away in some fancy PalmPilot, but in his mind. He had a photographic memory that had never failed him.

Reaching the elevator, he pressed for a car. Just as he stepped inside, he was aware that someone had slipped in behind him. The floor had appeared deserted a moment earlier.

"Sorry," a woman's voice apologized a second after he felt someone bump into him from behind.

Turning around, he was about to say something when he saw that it had been the woman's stomach that had made contact with him.

Rounded with child. The phrase came floating to him out of nowhere.

So did the smile that curved his lips ever so slightly. "That's all right."

Sherry looked down innocently at the bulk that

preceded her everywhere these days. She placed her hands on either side of the girth.

"Can't wait for this little darling to be born so I can move it around in a stroller instead of feeling as if I'm lifting weights every time I get up."

Because pregnancy, children and loved ones existed on an unknown plane, Sin-Jin could only vaguely nod at her words. A rejoining comment failed to materialize. The only thing he noted was, pregnant or not, the woman was extremely attractive.

His father had said there was no such thing as an attractive pregnant woman, but then, his father had demanded perfection in everything around him, if not in himself. The man was interested in ornamental women, not pregnant ones. Like a spoiled child in a toy store, his father had gone from one woman to another, marrying some along the way. He was vaguely aware that the man's tally stood at something like seven.

Or was it six? He'd lost count. The slight smile widened on Sin-Jin's lips, curving somewhat ironically.

Not bad, Sherry thought. The man was almost human looking when he smiled. She already knew that he was handsome. That much she'd gleaned while surfing the Internet for more than two hours, trying to piece together anything she could find on the man. She'd discovered that Owen was right. There wasn't anything on St. John Adair that didn't have to do with business. It was as if he disappeared into a black hole every night when he left the impressive edifice that bore his name.

It made her feel like Vicki Vale, on the trail of Batman.

Well, Batman was smiling, she thought. Perhaps not directly at her, but close enough.

Maybe Adair had a weak spot for pregnant women. It would be nice to be given an ace in the hole because of her condition for a change.

She took a deep breath, bracing herself. No time like the present.

Leaning around Adair, Sherry pressed the emergency stop on the elevator. The elevator hiccuped and came to an abrupt, jarring halt between the eighteenth and seventeenth floors.

The smile on his lips vanished instantly as a score of different scenarios crowded into his mind. Was he being threatened, kidnapped? There'd been two botched attempts at that in the past four years. He began to doubt the woman was pregnant. It made for a good disguise, put a man off his guard.

He was on his guard now. ''What the hell are you doing?''

Sherry's smile was sweetness personified as she looked up at him. ''I was wondering if you could give me a moment of your time, Mr. Adair.''

Chapter Two

For one heartbeat, there was nothing but silence within the elevator. Sin-Jin stared at the only other occupant in the car as if she had lost her mind. He wondered if she was dangerous in any sense of the word.

"Who *are* you?"

Sherry was ready for him. Opening her purse, she took out the press card that she'd carefully laid on top just before entering the multiwinged building that bore Adair's name. This was *not* the time to fumble through the various paraphernalia that she deemed indispensable and always dragged along with her.

She held her identification card aloft for Adair's perusal. And watched a transformation.

The unfriendly look on his face turned to something that, in a different era and country, would have reduced pagan worshipers to quivering masses of fear had Adair been their emperor, or, more probably regarded as their god. She felt a little unnerved herself.

Sherry shook herself loose from the hypnotic effect and squared her shoulders. Fierce expression or not, he wasn't about to make her back down.

Adair's glare was hot enough to melt the plastic on her ID. "You're a reporter?" It sounded like an offense second only to being a serial killer.

Damn, but she could see how he could strike fear into the hearts of those around him. She reminded herself that she wasn't afraid of anything except a magnitude-seven earthquake.

"Investigative," she informed him crisply, as if that fact took her out of the general pool that merited his disdain and elevated her to a higher plateau.

It didn't. Electric-blue eyes nearly disappeared into small, darkly lashed slits. "All right, then go investigate something."

The growled order only had her stiffening her backbone. She met him on his own battlefield, smiling sweetly. "I am. You."

"The hell you are." He reached past her to press the elevator release button only to have her hit the red stop button again. Stunned, he glared at her. "You will stop doing that." It was a command, brooking no disobedience, no dissent.

Her smile never faltered as she met his words with a condition. "I will if you promise to answer a few questions for me."

Mrs. Farley had pleaded with him to take on a bodyguard. Had even gone so far as to line up several for him to interview, but he'd then refused flatly, thinking it a waste. Now he wasn't all that sure. At least bodyguards would keep annoying reporters where they belonged. Away.

"I never make promises I have no intention of keeping." Again he pushed the button to restart the elevator and again she stopped it. "Look, lady—Mrs. Campbell—" he amended, exasperation evaporating the very air in his lungs.

"Right in the first place, wrong in the second," she informed him cheerfully, then suggested, "Why not just Sherry?"

She didn't think it possible, but his dark expression darkened even more.

"Because, 'just Sherry,' I don't intend to get that friendly with you." He hit the release button and the elevator made it to another floor before she abruptly halted it with a counterpunch. "You keep this up and the cable's liable to break. We'll wind up free-falling the rest of the way. That might be on your agenda, 'just Sherry,' but it's not on mine."

The glare he shot her bordered on filleting her nerves. She could see his underlings scattering and running for cover like so many Disney mice before the villainous cat in *Cinderella.* The thought did a lot to calm her nerves and made it difficult for her not to grin.

Sin-Jin's eyes slid to her belly. "Are you even pregnant?" It could have been a ruse used to allow her to gain access to his floor. In his experience, reporters were capable of all sorts of devious deceptions.

She surprised him by taking his hand and placing it on her distended abdomen. "Most definitely."

As if burned, Sin-Jin pulled his hand back. Although not soon enough. He'd felt the stirrings of new life beneath his palm. The child she was carrying had moved—probably on cue, he thought cynically.

What was a pregnant reporter doing here, lying in wait for him? He thought of the meeting he'd just left. "If this is about the Marconi merger—"

Sherry cut him short. "It's not," she told him. Raising her eyes to his face, she dug up all the charm she could muster. "It's about you."

Suspicion entered his eyes. He'd never had any use for reporters, feeding off the misery of others for their own ends. "What about me?"

"That's exactly what I want to find out. What about you? Nobody knows anything about Darth Vader, the Corporate Raider."

He winced inwardly at the label. If it was meant to flatter him, it missed its mark by a country mile. The limelight had never meant anything to him. Sin-Jin didn't do what he did for any sort of recognition. He did it because he was good at it, good at trimming fat off selected businesses and getting them to run more efficiently. Once he accomplished what he set out to do and the businesses were running at their maximum peak, he grew bored with them, selling them off to other corporations while he turned his attention to something else.

That this sort of thing attracted a great deal of attention and generated an almost obscene amount of money was without question. But it was never about the money. It never had been, perhaps because there'd always been so much of it when he was growing up. Every movement he'd ever made had been cushioned in it, as if somehow money could take the place of everything else that was deemed important in life. Like parental love and warm memories to draw on when things became difficult.

He'd had the best upbringing that money could buy. All needs taken care of, everything done in a utilitarian fashion. It was the kind of upbringing that could have produced an emotional robot, which was what his enemies had accused him of being.

If no one knew anything about him, it was for a reason. Because he wanted it like that. ''And it's going to remain that way,'' he informed her.

As he reached to bring the elevator back to life, she moved to block his access. ''Why?''

For just the smallest second, he almost forgot that they were stuck, suspended between the eighth and ninth floor like a yo-yo that had gotten tangled in its own string. The annoying woman who kept insisting on getting into his face had eyes that were probably the deepest shade of blue he'd ever seen. Undoubtedly, she used that to her advantage, just as she used her present condition.

''Does the word *privacy* mean anything to you?'' he demanded. ''Or is that particular term missing from the lexicon distributed to the ignoble fourth estate?''

''Ouch, they weren't kidding when they said you could fillet a person at ten paces with just your tongue.''

''No,'' he informed her tersely, ''they weren't.''

But rather than take offense at his words, she smiled, her face lighting up as if he'd just given her a ten-carat diamond instead of an insult.

She probably saw it as a challenge. He supposed he could relate to that. Challenges were what he responded to himself. The harder something was to obtain, the more he wanted to secure possession.

Somewhere in the back of his mind a question crept forward. How difficult would it be to possess the woman crowding him in the elevator?

The next instant Sin-Jin blanketed the thought, smothering it. She was someone else's wife or at the very least, someone's significant other. And unlike his father who reveled in it, he didn't poach on another man's land or try to win another man's woman if she captured his attention.

Satisfied that the verbal duel was over, Sin-Jin pressed the release button on the keypad only to have her reach for it again. The high school physics assurance that for every action there was a reaction teased his brain. Mr. Harris would have been happy that he'd come away with something from his class, he thought.

Rather than allow the annoying woman to bring the elevator to yet another teeth-jarring stop, Sin-Jin caught her by the wrist and held on tightly.

"The game is over."

Sherry raised her chin. The look in her eyes told him that she wasn't intimidated. He realized with a jolt that he found it arousing.

Man does not live by bread alone. Or, in his case, by corporate takeovers, he thought. Maybe it was time he got out a little instead of burning the midnight oil.

"What are you hiding, Mr. Adair?" Sherry wanted to know. Anyone so secretive had to have something he didn't want revealed. She felt her curiosity climbing. "What are you afraid of?"

Sin-Jin realized that he was still holding her wrist. Tentatively he released it, ready to grab it again if she tried to stop the elevator's descent. "Being on trial for justifiable homicide."

Humor, she liked that. Even if it was a little dark. Sherry smiled in response, aware that it threw him off. She liked that, too.

"Then I'll just have to make sure you don't do away with me, at least not until I get my story."

He edged closer to the doors, blocking any access she might have to the keypad in case she decided to make a lunge for it. "Tempting as the trade might be, I'm not prepared to give you a story in exchange for your fading out of my life."

The elevator came to a stop. "When will you be prepared?"

The doors opened. He saw the security guard sitting at the desk in the lobby. If this hounding reporter gave him any more trouble, he could turn her over to the man. "There's an old song, 'The Twelfth of Never.' I suggest you take your cue from the title."

With that, Sin-Jin got off.

Just as she began to follow Adair, the baby kicked. Hard. It momentarily took her breath away. Long enough for Adair to get far enough ahead of her.

"You can run, Adair, but you can't hide," she called after him.

Sin-Jin never broke stride and didn't bother looking over his shoulder. But his words hung in the air as he made his exit through the revolving doors.

"Watch me."

The glove had clearly been thrown down. Owen had been right. This was a definite challenge. Exhilaration filled her.

"I intend to do more than that, Adair," she murmured with a grin.

Two hours later, drained, Sherry flirted with the thought of just going home and crawling into her queen-size bed. By her count, she was down some ten hours of sleep in the past five days because her baby insisted on kickboxing for hours on end.

But tonight was her weekly Lamaze class and she hated to miss that. If nothing else, she could definitely use the camaraderie. Not to mention the fact that Rusty, her former cameraman and present coach, would be there. She could pick his brain about Adair. The man had a way of ferreting things out. If Rusty Thomas didn't know about something, it didn't bear knowing.

The practical side of attending her class was that she was a little more than a month away from her due date. A minor sense of panic was beginning to set in at the peripheral level. She needed all the preparation for the big event she could get.

Stopping home for a small dinner and a large pillow, Sherry changed her clothes to something even looser and more comfortable. Fifteen minutes later she was on the road again, driving to Blair Memorial where the classes were being held in one of the hospital's outlying facilities.

The cheerfully painted room was built to accommodate a hundred. Twenty couples had signed up. They were down to thirteen after the instructor, Lori O'Neill, had shown the birthing movie. Apparently there were miracles that were a little too graphic for some people to bear. Sherry liked the extra space. It made the gathering seem more like a club than a class.

Entering the class, her pillow tucked under her arm, Sherry looked around the area. Almost everyone was here. She nodded at couples she recognized by sight, if not by name. They were a cross section of life, she thought, being brought together by their mutual condition. In the group there was an independent film producer, a lawyer, three teachers, a doctor and an FBI agent, not to mention an assortment of other people.

She looked around for her group, two women she'd gotten close to in the last few weeks. Spotting Chris Jones and Joanna Prescott, Sherry made her way over to them. They had all been introduced to one another by Lori. The incredibly perky instructor had felt that the three women would form a strong bond, given that they were all single moms for one reason or another. Lori referred to them as The Mom Squad. Sherry rather liked that label.

"So, how was your week?" Joanna asked the moment Sherry came within earshot. Of the two of them, it was Joanna who could relate more closely to the woman she recognized as the former anchorwoman of the nightly news. Joanna, a high school English teacher, had lost her job for the same reason that had seen Sherry out the door of her studio. An unmarried pregnant woman was the elephant in the living room as far as the board of education was concerned. Rather than cause problems and be in the middle of an ugly trial that might affect her students, all of whom had rallied around her, Joanna had agreed to leave.

She knew the frustration that Sherry had dealt with.

"Don't ask." Sherry sighed the answer as she did her best to sink down gracefully. It wasn't an easy accomplishment. Of the three, Sherry was the furthest along.

And the largest, she thought ruefully. These days Sherry felt as if she was all stomach and very little else.

"The Mom Squad's all here, I see." Walking up to them, Lori placed an affectionate hand on Sherry's shoulder. She nodded at the two coaches who accompanied the other two women. "Hi, Sherry, where's your coach?"

Sherry glanced toward the doorway. Two couples came in, but no Rusty.

"He'll be along," she assured Lori. "Punctuality was never Rusty's strong suit."

"Well then, for your sake, I hope this baby turns out to be late," Lori teased.

Lori shifted, trying not to look too obvious. Her back was aching. And with good reason. She hadn't told the others yet but she'd found herself in the same delicate condition that they were in. Five months along, she wasn't showing too much yet. With any luck, she'd be one of those rare women who could hide inside of moderately loose clothing and never show.

The noise at the door had her turning to look. "Oh, more arrivals." About to go off and greet the newcomers, she paused for a final word with the trio. "We still on for ice cream after class, ladies?"

Chris and Sherry nodded. "Try and stop me," Joanna laughed. "I've been fantasizing about a mound of mint-chip ice cream all day."

"See you later," Lori promised before she hurried away.

Sherry glanced at her watch, wondering what was keeping Rusty. Class was almost starting. Thinking about what she wanted to ask her former cameraman, she leaned over toward Chris. Blond and vibrant, Chris Jones was not the kind of woman who came to mind when someone said FBI agent, but that was exactly what she was, having been part of the Bureau for over six years now.

"Chris, what do you know about St. John Adair?"

"If you're asking if the man has an FBI dossier, I wouldn't be able to answer that—" And then Chris smiled. "If he did."

Sherry made the natural assumption. "Which means he doesn't."

"Ruthless takeovers aren't a crime in themselves, except perhaps to the people who lose their jobs because of them." Chris cocked her head as if curious. One by one they'd each spilled their stories over various mounds of ice cream at Josie's Old-Fashioned Ice Cream Parlor. "Why do you want to know?"

Sitting cross-legged on the floor, Sherry pressed her hand to the small of her back, wondering if the perpetual ache she felt there was ever going to be a thing of the past. ''My editor wants me to do an in-depth piece on him. I actually cornered the man in his elevator today.''

''And?'' Joanna pressed.

Sherry frowned. ''Mr. Adair wasn't very cooperative. Didn't even volunteer his name, rank and serial number. I think if he had his druthers, he would have had me up against and wall and shot.''

Joanna nodded at the information. ''I've never seen anything written up about him. From what I've heard, he's really closemouthed.'' She glanced at Chris for confirmation. ''Maybe he's got some skeletons in his closet.''

Why else would someone be that secretive, Sherry wondered, nodding. She glanced again toward the doorway. No Rusty. ''That's what I'm thinking.''

''Well, if it makes a difference, none of them have gotten there by foul play. At least,'' Chris qualified, ''not to the Bureau's knowledge.'' She stopped and nodded toward the doorway. ''Hey, there's your coach.''

Without waiting for Sherry to turn around, Chris raised her hand and waved at the short, wiry man until he saw her. Raising a hand in response, he waved back and made his way over to the small, tight group.

Sherry sidled over to make room for him. Jerome Russell Thomas had been the first person to learn about her pregnancy, before her parents, even before Drew. They'd been out on a rare field assignment together, trying to corral a statement from a high-seated judge who had been brought up on bribery charges when she'd had to excuse herself. She'd barely made it to the ladies' room in time before her lunch, breakfast and whatever might have been left of her dinner the night before came up unceremoniously.

When she'd emerged from the ladies' room ten minutes later, sweaty and slightly green, Rusty was waiting for her just outside the door. One look at her and he'd asked her how far along she was. Her heated denial was short-lived in the face of his gruff kindness.

"My kid sister was the same shade of green that you are with her first," he'd told her matter-of-factly. "Couldn't keep anything down, not even water. Only thing she lived on was mashed potatoes and beef Stroganoff. You might want to try some."

Rusty had also stood by her when Drew had decided to pull his disappearing act on her and had been there for her when the studio had all but given her the bum's rush.

Having shown his true colors through the hard times, Rusty had seemed like the logical choice to be her coach. When she'd asked him, Rusty had protested vehemently at first, telling her that she would be far more comfortable if she had a woman as her coach. That *he* would be far more comfortable if she had a woman as her coach.

But Sherry had remained adamant, insisting she wanted him, and finally, he'd given in and agreed, grumbling all the way. She'd expected nothing less of him.

"Sorry I'm late. Had to fight off a horde of women at my door to get here," he cracked.

Given the truth of the matter, the only female in his life, other than the ones he worked with, was his dog, Blanca. Sherry didn't waste any time commenting on his fanciful excuse. Instead, the moment he dropped down beside her, she hit him with her question.

"What do you know about St. John Adair?"

Accustomed to her abrupt, greetingless greetings, Rusty paused to think.

"What everyone else knows. That he's one of the richest son-of-a-bitches around. I don't trust a man who looks that comfortable in a suit in ninety degree weather." Rusty never cracked a smile. "There's talk he's the devil. Why?"

She watched Lori work her way to the front of the room. They were getting ready to start. "Owen's giving me a crack at an investigative story."

Rusty filled in the blanks. It wasn't hard. He looked at her stomach, his meaning clear. "Couldn't he have started you out on something easier? Like finding out where Jimmy Hoffa's buried?"

Sherry shifted slightly. As if that could hide something. "Easy doesn't put you on the map."

He shrugged carelessly. "Neither does coming up to a dead end."

She didn't buy that. Although Lori was saying something to the gathering, Sherry lowered her voice, doing her best to appeal to Rusty. "You know everything there is to know about everything, including where all the bodies are buried. Tell me how I can get to him for a few minutes where he can't get away. Other than an elevator,'' she added.

''You always did know how to flatter a guy.'' It was a tall order, but not anything he wasn't up to. There was very little he wouldn't do for Sherry. In the vernacular of the old-timers who had taught him his trade, he considered Sherry Campbell one hell of a broad. ''Okay, I'll see what I can dig up for you, although it probably won't be very much.''

Sherry got herself into position, ready to begin. ''At this point, I'll settle for anything. I tried to corner him in the elevator but I couldn't get anything out of him.''

''Any man who can say no to you just isn't human.''

Touched, Sherry leaned over and kissed Rusty's leathery cheek. ''Thanks, Rusty. I needed that.''

Rusty tried not to blush. ''Shhh.'' He pointed to Lori. ''Teacher's talking. You'll miss something.''

She was still smiling at him. ''I'll always have you to fill me in.''

Rusty's blush deepened beneath the bronzed, craggy suntan.

Chapter Three

"Ladies, I have a confession to make."

Lori sank her long-handled spoon into the mound of whip cream atop her fudge-ripple sundae before looking up at the other three women seated with her in the ice-cream parlor booth.

The establishment, decorated to resemble something straight out of the early fifties, provided an informal atmosphere where they could each give voice to the concerns that were troubling them, concerns about the way their lives were about to everlastingly change because of the heart that beat beneath their own. It was something they all looked forward to far more than the classes that were to ready them for the upcoming big event.

"Let me guess," Chris interjected, deadpan. "You're not really a Lamaze instructor, you're actually an international spy.'' Not being able to hold it back any longer, Chris grinned as she glanced around at the others. ''Sorry, occupational habit. I've been bringing my work home with me a lot.''

Joanna nodded knowingly. ''Trust no one, right?'' A healthy spoonful of cookie-dough ice cream punctuated her declaration.

Chris acknowledged how good it felt to laugh about her work. So much of it revolved around darker elements. ''That's only a rule of thumb when you're checking out aliens on Sunday nights, Joanna.''

Sherry leaned forward. They were meandering again. That was usually a good thing as far as their conversations went, but Lori looked as if she had to get something off her chest. ''What's your big news, Lori?''

Lori let her spoon all but disappear into the dessert. Sherry noted that, unlike the rest of them, Lori had hardly eaten any of hers. A distant bell went off in her head, but for now she kept her suspicions on ice.

''Well,'' Lori blew out a breath, ''I don't know if it's big—'' She hesitated.

Chris was a firm believer in cutting to the chase. Even when she was trying to relax. ''Sure it is, otherwise you wouldn't be hemming and hawing. C'mon, woman, out with it.''

There was no putting this off. Even if Lori wanted to, it would be evident soon enough. And these women had become her friends. Initially, she'd been the one to encourage them to turn to her and one another. Now she needed them. Life certainly had an ironic bent to it.

Her glance swept around the square table. "I think that my ties to this little group are going to get stronger."

Joanna looked at her, slightly confused before a light slowly began to dawn. The light had already reached Chris, but before she could say anything, Sherry beat her to it. "You're pregnant."

Pressing her lips together, Lori nodded.

"And you don't think you and the dad are going to get together." It wasn't hard for Chris to fill in the blanks, given the nature of the expression of Lori's face.

"Not anymore." Lori looked down at her dessert. Rivulets of light brown were flowing down along the entire circumference of the tulip-shaped glass bowl, forming a sticky ring around the base. She dabbed at them with her napkin. "My husband is dead."

Chris looked at her sharply. "Oh, Lori, we're so sorry."

"Yes, I know. So am I," Lori said, her hand inadvertently covering her still-flat stomach, mimicking a motion she'd seen time and again in her classes. She tried to sound positive. "I'll be all right."

"Of course it will." Sherry could see that the woman didn't really want to talk about it, that what she wanted right at this moment was to have the unconditional support of her friends at a time in her life that could charitably be called trying.

Reaching out, she squeezed Lori's hand. When Lori looked in her direction, Sherry quipped, "So, how about those Dodgers?"

Laughing, the others took their cue, and the conversation drifted to all things light and airy, temporarily taking their minds away from the more serious areas of their lives.

A great deal of ice cream was consumed within the next hour.

The insidious ringing sound burrowed its way into the tapestry of her dreams, shredding the fabric before Sherry could think to snatch it back and save it for review once she was awake.

The instant her eyes were opened, the dream became a thing of the past.

The only thing she could remember was that it had created a warm haze of well-being within her. Something to do with a man loving her, caring for her, that was it. Instinctively she knew the man had been Drew during his better days, even though the face hadn't belonged to him.

Was it morning already?

The phone. That horrid ringing noise was coming from the phone, not her alarm clock.

With a huge sigh, Sherry groped for the receiver. It took her two tries to locate it. Her eyes were shutting again, refusing to surrender to the intruding morning. She tucked the receiver against her ear and the pillow.

"This better be good," she threatened.

By no stretch of the imagination was she now, or ever had been, a morning person. As far as she was concerned, God should have made sure that days began no earlier than eight o'clock, which was still pretty obscene in her book, but at least doable.

"Rise and shine, Cinderella. You told me to call when I had something."

Rusty. Rusty was talking in her ear.

Her eyes flew open. She struggled to defog her brain. "What do you have?"

"Not overly much," he warned her.

She knew better. Rusty wouldn't be calling her at this hour, whatever it was, if it was nothing. He didn't have a death wish.

"It's too early to play games, Rusty." Blinking, Sherry turned her head and tried to focus on her clock. It was barely five o'clock. No wonder she felt like death. "God isn't even up yet. Talk to me. What did you find out?"

"There's this mountain retreat. It belongs to someone else, somebody named Fletcher, but Adair likes to go to it just after he does a takeover—I won't say a successful takeover because when he's involved, they're all successful," he commented. "Going there is his way of celebrating." The raspy sound that passed for his laugh undulated through the phone lines. "Personally, if I had his kind of money, I'd be out on the town. Hell, I'd be out *buying* the town."

Still lying against her pillow, Sherry dragged her hand through her hair. "So he's shy, okay, we already know that. Where's this retreat located?"

"At the foot of the San Bernadino Mountains, just outside of Wrightwood."

She'd been to Wrightwood a couple of times herself. It was a small town, predominantly known for its noncommercial skiing. All the dedicated skiers went to Big Bear, which was located on the other side of Wrightwood. The former offered snow and gridlock during the winter months. Wrightwood offered scenery, charm and relative isolation. She could see Adair going there.

Sherry waited, knowing, even in her semiconscious state, that there was more.

Rusty paused dramatically. ''I managed to find out that Adair's going there this weekend. As a matter of fact, he's already on his way.''

Sherry took it for granted that what he was telling her was not common knowledge. If it was, Adair would be on his way to a media circus camped out on the front lawn. Given his personality, that would be the last thing he'd want.

She smiled to herself. Rusty never ceased to amaze her. The man was definitely a national treasure. She blessed the day she'd gone to bat with him with their former station manager when the man had wanted to terminate Rusty, saying he wasn't a team player. It had gained her a lifelong ally.

''I know that I shouldn't be asking this, Rusty, but how did you find this out?''

She could almost hear his smile as it spread over his generous mouth. He had a nice smile, she thought absently.

''Mrs. Farley keeps religious notes.''

The name was vaguely familiar, but at five in the morning, nothing was overly clear. ''And she is?''

''His secretary. Has been for years. As a matter of fact, he brought her with him when he first came to SunCorp.'' That was what the corporation had been called before he'd changed the name to Adair Industries. ''From what I've gathered, Adair trusts her the way he doesn't trust anyone else.''

That would have been the lioness at the gate, Sherry thought. The woman who hadn't allowed her to see Adair. She'd asked the secretary for an audience with Adair before resorting to the elevator trick. There hadn't seemed to be anything remarkable about Edna Farley. Obviously she hadn't looked closely enough. "Interesting. And you got these notes how?"

"I know a lot of people, Sherry. Some of them don't stray more than five feet from their computers at any given time."

Hackers, he'd used hackers. Well, whatever made the world go around, she mused. "Got a location on this retreat?"

He chuckled. She knew better than to doubt him. "Is the Pope Catholic?"

"Last time anyone checked." Awake now, she opened the drawer of the nightstand beside her bed and pulled out a pad and pencil. "Okay, shoot."

Rusty hesitated. "Look, instead of my giving the directions to you over the phone, why don't I just come over in a couple of hours and drive you over there myself?"

Rusty had his own job. She knew for a fact that he couldn't afford to take time off. The station manager would be all over him if he did. "You've already done enough, Rusty." There'd been concern in his voice. She found it sweet but shackling. "I can take care of myself."

Rusty huffed. "In case you haven't noticed, you're pregnant."

She hated the fact that people viewed her differently because of her condition. Of all people Rusty should have known better. "Being pregnant doesn't mean I can't see over the steering wheel, Rusty, or that I've suddenly forgotten how to take corners."

He laughed gruffly. "I've seen how you drive, Campbell. They should have taken away your keys the second anyone found out you were expecting."

"Sweet of you to worry, Rusty, but I can take it from here. Just give me the directions."

He knew better than to argue with her. When it came to being stubborn, he'd learned his first week on the job that Sherry had no equal. He rattled off the directions, including which freeway exits she was to take and for how long. He prided himself on being thorough.

"If you change your mind about going alone, you know where to find me. I'll be the one on the arm of the sexiest cover model in the room."

"That's just how I'll expect to find you." Laughing, she hung up.

With a sigh, Sherry dug her fists in on either side of her and then pushed herself up into an upright position.

Adair.

The memory hit her like a thunderbolt. The face of the man in her dream, the one who was supposed to have been Drew, had belonged to Adair.

Her eyes widened before she dismissed the thought. Her brain had obviously taken recent events and combined two areas of her life. Either that, or she was hallucinating. The only thing that Adair had going for him was piles of money. Okay, that and looks, she amended. Neither of which meant anything to her. The next time she was going to trust a man, he was going to have to be strong, sensitive and caring.

A sense of humor wouldn't hurt, either. As for looks, well, she already knew what that was worth. Pretty faces, like as not, usually were the domain of shallow, vacant people. Drew was living proof of that.

With yet another deep sigh, Sherry got off the bed and went to the bathroom. The first visit of many today, she thought wearily.

He liked it here.

Liked the massive wood-framed rooms, the sparse furnishings, the wide-open spaces, both inside and out. He'd driven most of the night to get here after his late meeting with his lawyers to finalize the deal he'd been working on. It was worth it.

Sin-Jin looked through the bay window that faced the mountain and the landing pad where his private helicopter stood, waiting his pleasure. He wouldn't be using it today. He wanted nothing more than to stay here.

There was no doubt about it. There was something bracing about being alone in the wilderness.

Of course, he didn't attempt to delude himself that he was the thriving descendent of some savvy, resourceful frontier backwoodsman. He liked his creature comforts along with his solitude. Although he had to admit that he had toyed with the idea of not having a phone here. But in the end his sense of practicality had won over his need to be alone. The compromise was that only Mrs. Farley had his phone number here.

He trusted her implicitly. She wouldn't do anything to jeopardize his privacy. Privacy had become paramount for him. That was why the cabin he chose to stay in was registered to John Fletcher in the county books. No one suspected he was here today.

Mrs. Farley and he went way back. Far further than anyone suspected. Certainly a lot further than his years as a corporate raider. Other than his uncle, Edna Farley had been the first person to make a positive impact in his life, the first person who had made him feel that he mattered.

Who knew what path his life would have taken if not for her, he mused.

He owed her, owed her a great deal. Though not very vocal, he'd told her as much years ago. All she had ever asked of him was to let her earn her keep. He would have been more than willing to set her up with a lifetime trust fund in any place of her choice. She would have been set for life, but she'd chosen to work at his side. That was typical of her.

He had to admit, he rather liked that. In a way she was the mother his own mother had never been, although Edna Farley never blatantly displayed maternal feelings. They were alike that way, each shut inside with their own emotions. But she took care of him nonetheless. As he did her.

Sin-Jin looked at the gray flagstone fireplace, debating building a fire. The air was nippy up here, a hundred miles away from where he usually resided. It was barely fall, but cold weather found its way faster to this part of Southern California. There was no snow on the mountains yet, but prospects looked good, he thought. The local shopkeepers would be happy.

Maybe someday he'd retire here, he mused. It would be an idyllic life. His mouth curved. As if he could stand a life with no challenges for more than a few days.

The sound of barking in the distance alerted him. Striding across the hardwood floor, Sin-Jin went directly to his gun cabinet and took out a rifle. As he moved to the front door, he loaded the weapon. That was Greta barking. His Irish setter was his flesh-and-blood alarm system and as far as he was concerned, she did a far more effective job than any state-of-the-art laser beams. There were other advantages as well. A high-tech system couldn't curl up at his feet in the evening and look up at him with soulful brown eyes that helped to ease the building tension of his everyday life.

Pulling the door open, Sin-Jin looked around. The woods were some three hundred feet to his right, but from this vantage point, he saw nothing.

"What is it, Greta?"

At the sound of his voice, the barking increased. As he listened, he placed the direction of origin. It was coming from several yards away. Sin-Jin strode toward the sound, his fingers wrapped around his weapon, ready for anything.

Anything except for what he found.

It was that woman again, that reporter who'd jumped into the elevator with him the other day and tried to waylay him for a story.

Damn it, how the hell did she find this place?

He scowled as he went toward her. She wore a

white parka that hung open around her. He doubted that she could even come close to zipping it up around her stomach.

Something Campbell, that was it. Cheryl? No, Sherry.

He grew angrier with every step he took. She had the face of an angel and the body of a lumbering bear all primed for hibernation. Why wasn't she hibernating?

''You're trespassing!'' he called out to her. ''What the hell are you doing up here?''

Sherry struggled to catch her breath. The all-terrain vehicle she'd borrowed from a friend had decided that it wasn't altogether happy traversing this terrain and had given up the ghost about half a mile down the road. Walking had never been a problem for her, even while carrying around the extra pounds that her baby had brought with it, but this particular half mile had all been uphill. The dog appearing out of nowhere hadn't exactly helped matters any. Her heart was still pounding wildly. Luckily the dog had decided to be friendly.

''Right now, having car trouble,'' Sherry managed to get out.

Yeah, right. You'd think that someone who wrote for a living would be more original than that. ''If you expect me to believe that—''

''Go see for yourself.'' Turning, Sherry pointed behind her down the mountain. ''It's about half a mile down the road.''

He had half a mind to call the sheriff and have her arrested. That would put the fear of God into her. Fuming, Sin-Jin glared at her. The woman was panting. He eyed her stomach. Her whole body seemed to be vibrating from the effort it had taken to get here.

"Are you out of your mind?" he demanded. Pregnant women were supposed to stay near hospitals, not hike up mountainsides.

"Probably." She stopped to draw in more air. Her lungs were finally beginning to feel as if they weren't about to explode. She tried to smile and succeeded only marginally. "I've been accused of that on occasion."

Sin-Jin glanced down at Greta. The dog was prancing around the woman who kept insisting on intruding into his life. It was as if Greta and the reporter were old friends. The barking, now that he thought about it, had been the friendly variety, the kind he was apt to hear when Greta wanted to play. Obviously the animal didn't see the woman as a threat.

He wondered if Greta was getting old.

Sherry tried to wet her lips and discovered that she couldn't. Her mouth felt as dry as dust. "I hate to trouble you, but would you mind getting me a glass of water?"

"Yes." Disgusted, Sin-Jin paused. It would serve the woman right if he sent her on her way just as she was. He sincerely doubted that there was anything wrong with her car. But she was obviously pregnant, and there were beads of perspiration along her brow despite the cold temperature. The walk up here, for whatever reason, had cost her. He glanced back at the cabin. Sin-Jin didn't relish the idea of taking her in there. "I don't suppose you want it out here."

Sherry was beginning to feel very wobbly, as if her legs were turning to the consistency of cotton after being soaked in water. "If you don't mind, I'd like to sit down." She glanced at her surroundings and second-guessed what he was about to say. "Preferably not on a rock."

She raised her eyes to his, the blueness assaulting him. In the light of day they looked even more intense than they had in the elevator. There was something really unsettling about the way she looked at him. His thoughts came to an abrupt halt as he gazed into her eyes.

Probably just the altitude getting to him, Sin-Jin reasoned.

"What a surprise," he muttered. "All right, come on." He waved her forward. "But once you're rested, you're going back."

She didn't bother trying to keep up. Walking was now a challenge.

"My car died," she reminded him.

"I'm pretty handy with a car. I'll get it going." There was no room for doubt in his voice. He glanced over his shoulder to see if she'd heard him. Her mouth was curved. "Why are you smiling?"

"I've learned something about you already." She struggled not to huff as she followed. "I don't recall reading anywhere that you were handy with cars."

Sin-Jin blew out a breath, saying nothing. Instead he glanced at Greta, who was prancing excitedly from foot to foot as she ran alongside of the woman, only to backtrack and then begin again. She gave the impression of trying to shepherd the reporter into his cabin.

"Traitor," he muttered under his breath.

Chapter Four

Trying to contain his anger, Sin-Jin slammed the door the second the woman was inside. The Irish Setter jumped. Greta looked up at him accusingly. The feeling was mutual.

Taking out the ammunition, he parked his rifle in the corner and deposited the shells on the coffee table. ''You're lucky I don't call the sheriff.''

Sherry took in her surroundings. The ceiling in the living area was vaulted, with heavy wooden beams running across it. The look of massive wood was everywhere. It was a man's retreat, built by a man for a man. If Adair brought women to his friend's cabin, they hadn't left any telltale marks. Even the framed photograph on the mantel had no people in it, just a scenic panorama of what looked like the Lake Tahoe area.

She turned to look at him, fighting an odd wave of discomfort unlike any she'd experienced in the past nine months, a passage of time marked with a great many moments of discomfort. Sherry tried to focus on his face. His expression was as cold as the weather outside.

"You didn't call the sheriff because you don't want to be laughed at, Mr. Adair." She pointed toward the framed photograph. "Is that Lake Tahoe?"

"Yes." Impatience echoed in his voice. "As for calling the sheriff—"

Feeling suddenly woozy, Sherry collapsed in the nearest chair without bothering to ask if she could. It took effort to complete her thought. "Not many people would see their way clear to your feeling threatened by a pregnant woman."

He looked down at her and glared. The woman was making herself right at home, wasn't she? "You don't threaten me, Ms. Campbell, you annoy me."

As if to defuse the moment, Greta eased herself into the space formed by her arm and the chair, the setter's indication clear. She wanted to be petted. Sherry obliged the dog, taking comfort in the soothing act.

"Why? Because I'm trying to find out more about you than what can be read in those lackluster press releases your corporation issues?"

He strode into the kitchen, which was just off the living room and turned on the tap. "Exactly. This is a very public world we live in. I'm just trying to maintain a shred of privacy in it." Holding the filled glass of water in front of him, he crossed back to her. ''Used to be a man's right.'' He thrust the glass toward her. ''I'd like to go back to those times.''

Feeling suddenly unbelievably shaky, Sherry took the glass in both hands and drank deeply. She started to feel better. Whatever had been wrong a moment ago had passed, thank God. She was herself again. Something, she figured, Adair wouldn't be overly thrilled about.

Her mouth curved.

''You're right—it is a public world we live in, when almost everyone's life can be laid bare with the right keystrokes on the computer. The Internet is an endless font of information—yet there isn't anything about you.'' Her mouth dry, she took another long sip, letting her words sink in. ''It's almost as if you didn't exist outside of the nine to five business world.''

He thought about the past week. He'd barely had time to come home and change. It felt as if he hadn't slept at all. ''It's hardly nine to five.''

She realized that generalization didn't apply to him. ''All right nine to midnight. The point is—'' still petting the dog with one hand while holding on to the glass with the other, she moved slightly forward on the chair ''—who are you?''

The warmth in the cabin was imprinting itself on the woman's cheeks. Sin-Jin wondered how he could be annoyed and attracted at the same time. No doubt about it, he definitely needed to get out more.

''The point is, business takes up all my time and who I am is my business.''

The man was good, she'd give him that. He'd probably drive a lawyer crazy under cross-examination on the stand. ''Nicely put, Mr. Adair. You know how to use words to your advantage.''

Sin-Jin narrowed his eyes. ''If I did, you wouldn't be here.''

''Speaking of here,'' she gestured around the cabin, ''how is coming here business?''

Enough was enough. He shouldn't even be talking to her. ''I think you've asked enough questions.''

It was an interesting phenomenon. The more Adair scowled, the more at ease she seemed to feel. ''We'll put it to a vote.'' She glanced down at the Irish setter at her side. ''How about you, dog?''

An unfamiliar possessiveness came over him. ''Her name's Greta.''

Sherry nodded at the backhanded introduction. ''Even better. The personal touch.'' She looked into the setter's eyes. ''How about you, Greta? Do you think I've asked enough questions? No?'' She looked up at Adair, the essence of cheerfulness. ''That settles it. The vote's two to one—I already know how you're voting—for me to continue.''

Not that he wasn't amused in some strange, abstract sort of way, but it was time to cut this short. ''In this case, might makes right.''

She raised her eyebrows innocently. ''You're planning on Indian wrestling me?''

''No, I plan on carrying you to your car if necessary, fixing said car *if necessary,* and sending you back on your way.''

She twisted around to look at him. ''You really know how to fix cars?''

He put his hands on the back of the chair, debating

slanting it just enough to urge the woman to her feet. "Don't change the subject."

She'd come too far to be sidetracked now. Even though that strange feeling was back, she couldn't be deterred from her purpose. "That *is* the subject—*you* are the subject." He might not realize it, but she was picking things up about him. "What else do you know?"

The smattering of patience that he'd temporarily uncovered was gone. "I know when to end a conversation, something you apparently do not."

Time to switch tactics. She looked around. "Your friend has good taste."

The comment was out of left field, catching him short. "What?"

"Your friend," she repeated with emphasis. "The man who this cabin belongs to. John Fletcher," she added for good measure. "He has good taste."

The statement almost made him smile. Sin-Jin looked around, as if seeing it for the first time through someone else's eyes.

"Yes," he finally allowed, "he does." He looked at the half-empty glass of water she was still holding. "Are you finished with that?"

"Not yet." To prove it, she took another long sip. For some reason it just made her hotter. "You know, it's true what they say, about mountain water," she added when he looked confused. "I'm a tap water person myself, but there is a difference." She held the glass aloft as if to underscore her point.

Sin-Jin leaned his hip against another chair, his arms crossed before him as he regarded her. "Do you ever stop talking?"

"Feel free to jump in anytime." Her grin was wide and inviting and for a moment, managed to sneak in through a crack. He found himself being drawn in.

"I—" Stopping, Sin-Jin shook his head and laughed. She'd almost had him for a second. "That was transparent."

Undaunted, she shrugged. "Sometimes it works. Most people find me easy to talk to."

Yes, he supposed he could see that. But there was another factor involved. "When would they ever get a chance?"

She cocked her head, her eyes warm, coaxing. "All you have to do is start. Once you do, I'll shut up."

But better people than she had tried to worm their way into his world and get close to him. He'd stopped each in their tracks. Other than with Mrs. Farley, all his relationships were hallmarked by a distance, a space that none were allowed to cross.

"Sorry, Ms. Campbell, but I don't intend to tell you anything about myself."

She wasn't going to go away empty-handed, and something was better than nothing. There was no telling how one thing could lead to another. "All right, then tell me about John Fletcher. How long have you two been friends? When did you meet him? Did he go to the same school as you did?"

He felt as if he was being shelled with torpedoes. "I value my privacy and John values his." His expression was unshakable. "We're leaving it at that."

She stared at him for a long moment, reading her own meaning into his words. "Oh."

"What do you mean, 'oh?'"

"Just that. 'Oh.'"

The word was even more pregnant than she was. Visions of a headline rose in his mind. He wasn't about to drop it until she laid his fear to rest. "What are you implying?"

Her smile was easy, kind. Sin-Jin had no idea that there could be so many layers involved in such a simple action as the curving of the lips. "Now who's asking questions?"

Irritation sealed itself to frustration. "I have a right to ask questions if the subject concerns me."

"I thought you weren't going to be a subject." She would have been enjoying this more if part of her wasn't beginning to feel like a can of tuna fish being cracked apart with a rusty can opener.

He blew out a breath. As much as he hated drawing people into his life, maybe he should be calling the sheriff. "Has anyone ever told you that you're infuriating?"

If she only had a nickel…

"Occasionally," she said, tongue in cheek. "It usually happens when I stumble across a secret they don't want to let out."

"There is no secret to let out." He almost shouted the words at her.

Sherry pressed the issue just a little, although she had pretty much decided what his answer was going to be, and that she believed it. "Then you and this John Fletcher are not in a relationship?"

"No."

She was the soul of innocence when she asked, "And you're not gay?"

Damn it, just because there wasn't a string of women in his wake… "Of course I'm not gay," he shouted. "I wouldn't have found you attractive if I were."

That caught her by surprise. She hadn't felt remotely attractive for months now. Pregnant whales were not deemed attractive, except perhaps by other whales. Desperate other whales.

"You find me attractive?"

"Yes," he shouted again, then lowered his voice, "in a very irritating sort of way. Now, if you're finished with your water…" Not giving her time to answer, he took the glass out of her hand and put it squarely on the table. "I think it's time you showed me where this car of yours allegedly died."

Taking her arm to help her to her feet, Sin-Jin was surprised at how much resistance met the offer.

A beat before he took the water from her, she'd felt something awful happening. She looked up at him with wide eyes. "I don't think I can do that."

"And why is that?"

Spacious or not, the room began to feel as if it closed in on her and there was this awful pain emanating from the center of her body. "Because I think my water just broke."

He was almost disappointed. You'd really think a reporter could do better than that. "Ms. Campbell, I wasn't born yesterday or the day before that."

She was having trouble breathing. "I don't think that when you were born…is going to be an issue, but this baby…wants to be born…today."

She almost had him believing that something was

wrong. Except that he knew better. He looked at her icily. "How convenient."

"Not...really." Convenient would be if she could get someone else to give birth to this baby for her.

The hitch in her voice had him pausing. He was beginning to have his doubts at how accomplished an actress she actually was. "You're serious."

She sucked air in, trying desperately to remember what it was that Lori had said. The last eight weeks of classes seemed to vanish from her brain as if they'd never taken up space there. "Yes."

"You came up here on your due date?" The woman really was crazy.

Sherry wished that she'd listened to all those people who'd cautioned her about being careful, even though it went against her nature. "No...I came up here...almost a month away...from my due day."

Okay, then they had nothing to be concerned about. Taking her hand again, he made a second attempt to get her to her feet. "Well, then—"

She winced and collapsed back into the chair. Liftoff had existed for only three inches. She was positive that she felt a contraction. A hard one. "Apparently...they don't...issue calendars...along with... uteruses."

Since he couldn't get her to her feet, Sin-Jin sank down beside the chair, deciding for the moment to play along and give her the benefit of the doubt. No one could change color like that at will, no matter how good they were. She was definitely pale.

"Exactly what is it that you're feeling?" He wanted to know.

Words failed her. "A whole bunch...of things I'd

rather not…be feeling right now.'' She looked at him, a mild panic setting in and rising up to her eyes. She could see he didn't believe her. Sherry pressed her lips together, doing her best to explain. ''I feel like…I'm a tube of toothpaste that…someone's trying to squeeze the…last drop out of.''

He laughed shortly. ''If that's a sample of how you write, I suggest you change your profession.''

But even as he said it, the woman squeezed his hand so tightly the blood felt as if it would stop flowing. He started having doubts that she was doing this for his benefit. Early labors weren't entirely unheard of.

Here came another one. ''I'll...do a...revision... on it later. Is there…a doctor close by?'' The words were coming out in short pants. She hated this.

Sin-Jin thought of the small clinic that he'd anonymously funded. Its main function was to care for injured skiers, patching them up just enough to send them on to regular facilities that were far better equipped to handle emergencies. It was run by two physicians. ''There's a clinic about twenty miles from here.''

She gripped his hand harder. Why wasn't that making the pain go away? ''No…I mean *close*…like twenty feet…away.''

Sympathy began to stir. He'd never been one not to be moved by suffering. ''You're panicking.''

She tried to smile. The effort wasn't entirely successful. ''What was your…first…clue?''

He knew a little about what she was going

through. "Look, if you are in labor, you've got a long way to go before the baby's born."

A lot he knew. It felt as if the baby was trying to tear its way out of her with the jaws of life. And then hope nudged forward on the wings of irrationality. "You're not...a...closet doctor...are you?"

Part of him still couldn't help wondering if she was pulling this stunt just to find out more information about him. He'd had some medical training, but she didn't need to know that. At least, not yet.

"No, but haven't you heard the horror stories about women being in labor for seventy-two hours?"

The women in her office had converged around her, sharing their experiences and making her feel that giving birth was a torture second only to being drawn and quartered during the Spanish Inquisition. Joining the Lamaze class was her way of trying to placate her own fears.

"I've got...a horror story...of...my own. Giving...birth without...a doctor."

He looked at her pointedly, his voice firm. "You're not giving birth."

"I know my...own body," she gasped. "It's expelling the...foreign body...within...in this case, a ba—BEE!"

He winced as she suddenly jackknifed forward and shouted the last syllable in his ear. Sin-Jin could see the perspiration along her brow increasing.

He looked around, thinking. "Okay, let's say for the sake of argument that you are in some kind of accelerated labor—"

She felt as if she was being crushed from several different directions at once. Was this normal?

"I...don't want...to...argue, I want...this...to be over with." She gripped his hand even harder, trying to pull together what strength she had. "Are you...*sure*....there isn't someone...you can...call?"

Sin-Jin made his decision. She was on the level. But he sincerely doubted the situation was as urgent as she believed it was.

"C'mon," he tucked his hand under her arm. "I'll drive you to the clinic."

But even as he tried to get her to her feet, Sherry's knees buckled. She wound up sinking to the floor in a less-than-graceful movement. "I don't...think there's...time."

"You're serious." This time it wasn't a question, it was a resigned statement.

She thought she knew what he was thinking, hoping. Right now she wished he was right. "I don't...want...a...story this...badly."

"Okay, I believe you." Still on his knees beside her, Sin-Jin reached over to the sofa and pulled down the blanket that was slung over the arm. He spread it out on the floor as best he could while supporting her against him. "Let's get this jacket off you." Moving as swiftly as he could, he stripped the parka from her. It was drenched with perspiration. That clinched it. It wasn't an elaborate ruse. No one could perspire like that on cue. He pulled a cushion off and placed it at the edge of the blanket for her head.

She sagged against him. "What...are you going...to...do?"

He brushed the hair from her forehead before gently moving her toward the blanket. "Nothing, you're the quarterback in this. I'm just going to be the wide receiver, catching the football when you release it.''

She blew as a contraction closed its jaws around her and then finally released. ''You...play...football?''

''Played,'' Sin-Jin corrected. As he began to rise, Sherry caught his hand, her eyes widening. ''I'm just going to wash my hands.''

She watched his every move as he crossed to the kitchen. She was putting her fate into the hands of a man she and the world knew next to nothing about, except that he was ruthless when necessary. It wasn't a ringing endorsement. ''Do...you know...what you're...doing?''

He washed his hands quickly. ''Probably more than you do.'' Drying off, he crossed back to her.

''How?''

He shook his head. ''Don't you ever stop being a reporter?''

The contraction abated, allowing her to draw air back into her lungs. She was almost giddy from the respite. And then another began to gallop toward her, harder and faster than before. ''Right now...I'm being a...scared...woman...about to give...birth...a hundred miles from nowhere...in a cabin...with a man...known as the Darth Vader...of industry.''

Feeling sorry for her, he opened the door to his privacy just a crack. ''I've had a little medical training.''

He was trying to make her comfortable, she realized. ''How...little?''

He'd been premed for a while, actually toying with

the idea of becoming a doctor before he discovered that he had a truer calling. ''Enough.''

Sherry groped around either side of her, crumpling the blanket beneath white knuckles. ''Okay…I'm going to…trust…you.''

''Don't see that you have much of a choice,'' he told her gruffly.

He certainly wished he had. This wasn't the way he'd envisioned his day when he got up this morning. The cup of coffee he'd poured himself just before Greta had begun barking was still standing on the table, stone cold now, reminding him how, despite his best efforts, he had little control over life.

A sense of panic washed over her. Maybe this was a bad idea. What if something went wrong? This was a baby she was about to produce, not a contract. What did Darth Vader know about birthing babies? ''Are you sure…there isn't…time?''

Rocking back on his heels, he regarded her quietly. ''You tell me.'' There was another option. ''I could get you into the chopper and—''

She blinked. ''Chopper?''

''My helicopter.'' He nodded toward the rear of the cabin. ''It's on a landing pad a few yards from the house.''

He wasn't a man, he was a superhero. She tried to focus on his face, the perspiration dripping into her eyes making it hard to see. ''You fly…too?''

''Yes.'' If he was going to do this, he had to hurry. ''Look, no more questions. Are you up to a trip? I can have you back at the hospital—'' His statement was cut short as Sherry grabbed his hand again and screamed. ''I guess not. Okay, looks like the floor show's going to be here.'' He rolled up his sleeves. ''What did you say your first name was?''

Panting again, she held her hand up until the contraction lessened. ''Sherry.''

''Sherry,'' he repeated, nodding. ''All right, we're going to get through this, Sherry. Just remember, you're not the first woman to have her baby outside a hospital.''

He was talking to her. She knew he was talking, but his voice kept fading in and out. Sherry shook her head, trying to focus, trying to hear what he was saying. But everything was fading, being stuffed headlong into a large, dark cylinder.

And then a curtain fell and she heard and saw nothing. Fear was her only companion and it was about to swallow her up whole.

Chapter Five

The acrid odor assaulted her senses, rudely pushing its way into the black abyss and grabbing hold of her. Startled, trying to get away from the smell, Sherry rose to the surface, aware that she was twisting her head from side to side.

She opened her eyes and moaned a second before the pain came again, twice as strong as before and three times as overwhelming.

"What happened?" she gasped, coughing.

Sin-Jin kept the opened ammonia capsule by her nose a moment longer, just in case.

"You fainted," he answered matter-of-factly. She'd done more than that. She'd given him one hell of a scare. He wasn't sure if she'd just fainted or if the situation was actually far more dire. She'd remained unconscious for almost five minutes. "Don't do that again."

With wavering strength she pushed his hand away from her face. "I'll do...my best..." Her eyes flew open, looking like giant blue cornflowers searching for the sun. "Oh, God, oh, God, oh, God."

He tossed aside the capsule. "Another one?"

"Well...I'm not...praying to you... Don't you have...anything to...knock me out?"

"Other than my fist? No." He tried not to give in to the feeling of helplessness that was hovering over him. It wasn't an emotion he welcomed. "Hang in there."

About to prep her as best he could, Sin-Jin paused, hesitating even as he knew it was foolish. But privacy was such an issue with him that invading another's, no matter how noble the reason, just didn't seem right without permission.

As he picked up the edge of her denim jumper, he looked up at her. "Sorry."

The sentiment was genuine. In a haze comprised of pain, disorientation and jagged fear, Sherry was still moved by what she would have termed old-world courtliness in this impersonal world. Sin-Jin Adair wasn't just some coldhearted bastard who made his living gutting other people's dreams. There was far more to him than that.

If only she was in her right mind to make mental note of it.

She struggled to keep ahead of the pain that insisted on squeezing her within its jaws. Sherry bit her lip to keep the scream back, then nodded. There was a time for modesty, but she'd gone way past that now.

"Go ahead... Do what you have...to do."

Sin-Jin pushed up her jumper and got her ready to deliver her baby. The woman was fully dilated. ''My God, you're crowning.''

It was a familiar term, but if her soul had depended on it, she couldn't have said what it meant. ''Is that…a good thing?''

He did his best to sound encouraging. Behind him he could hear Greta pacing back and forth like a worried relative in a maternity waiting room.

''Means that this should be over with soon.'' Though he recalled all the particulars, he'd never actually attended a birth. He capped the uneasiness that tried to push forward. ''I see the head.''

A head. There had to be more, right? It felt like there was a convention going on inside of her and everyone was trying to push their way out the fire exit at the same time.

''Anything…else?''

''Not yet.''

She heard him doing things but had no idea what. It didn't matter. All that mattered was getting rid of this pain.

''I'm…passing…an elephant, there's…got to be…more.''

She looked fully ready to go. He glanced up at her face. ''Are you ready to push?''

Push, that meant this would be over soon, right? ''Ever since…this started.''

Sin-Jin took a breath, bracing himself. Hoping nothing was going to go wrong. ''Okay, on the count of three.''

His words echoed in her head. ''You're going…to push with…me?''

Even out of her head, she was still questioning things. It made him wonder how she'd gotten pregnant in the first place. "No, just take the credit when it's done."

She blinked, trying to focus on him. "A...sense of...humor?"

He lifted his shoulders in a half shrug. "I find it helps when things are tense."

Tense. That meant dangerous. Was her baby in danger? She tried to swallow, and it felt as if her throat was sticking to itself. "Are they?"

He heard the mounting panic. The last thing he needed right now was for her to give in to that. "Don't worry, I know what I'm doing," he assured her again. "My uncle was a doctor."

Had she had the energy, she would have asked about his uncle, about the rest of his family now that he'd allowed that to slip out. But her head began to swirl dangerously. It was all she could do to keep from passing out from the pain again. It was all around her now, like a giant steel vise.

Sin-Jin crossed his fingers that, like everything else she seemed to have done so far, she could get through this part quickly. "Okay, one, two, three—push!"

Gathering all her strength together, Sherry leaned as far forward as she could and pushed with all of her might. Heat assaulted her and she felt as if she was being pulled in two opposite directions. Panting, she fell back.

"Is it...out...yet?"

If only, he thought. "No, not yet."

She wanted to cry. This wasn't fair. It wasn't fair

that she was going through this and the man whose baby this was, who had broken her heart, wasn't even going to feel so much as a twinge. He'd moved on to another relationship, leaving her to handle all this by herself. She wanted Drew's head on a platter.

"Why...not?"

Because didn't seem enough of an answer, although that was what came to mind. "Because it doesn't go that fast."

She struggled to get air into her lungs. "It should. Who...made the...rules? Oh, God—"

He knew the signs by now. Her body was going rigid. There was no way for her to relax, even though it would be easier on her if she could.

"Okay, again." Sin-Jin watched her face intently as he issued the order. "One, two, three—push!" Sherry was already pushing before he reached the third number. He was afraid she was going to rupture something. "You've got to pace yourself, Sherry. Push when I tell you to push."

She looked at him accusingly, her lashes damp with perspiration. Maybe he'd like to trade places. "God, but...you are...bossy."

"I'm right." His voice left no room for argument. She was stiffening again. It wouldn't be long now. "All right, one, two—"

She shook her head, exhausted beyond words. "No, I can't...I just can't."

This wasn't a time to bail out. "Yes," he insisted firmly, "you can."

How dare he stand there, issuing orders, telling her what she was capable of? He was on the safe side of this torture rack. ‘‘How…many…babies have you…pushed…out?’’

‘‘I didn’t say this was easy, but you can’t stay pregnant forever.’’

She could feel the tears gathering. One trickled down her cheek, skimming the outline of her ear. ‘‘Not forever…just a little…longer. I can’t—’’

Abandoning his post at one end, Sin-Jin moved until he was close to her face. He took out his handkerchief and dried the path the tear had taken.

‘‘Yes,’’ he told her, his voice gentle, ‘‘you can. You’re a damn strong woman, Sherry Campbell. This is going to be in your past soon enough. Now do it for the baby.’’

She bit her lip again, trying to hold everything at bay. She could feel forces beyond her control undulating downward. ‘‘One…for the…gipper?’’

He laughed shortly. ‘‘Something like that.’’ With that he returned to where he felt he could do the most good. ‘‘Okay, now push!’’

With her last remaining ounce of strength, Sherry scooted her elbows in close to her body, propped herself up, and through clenched teeth almost shrieked out, ‘‘Okay.’’ Screwing her eyes shut tight, she pushed for all she was worth.

His hands in position between her legs, a sense of amazement skimmed over him as the small being began to emerge. As he shared in the miracle, a sensation like no other materialized within his chest.

‘‘You’re doing great, Sherry. The head’s coming.’’ He sucked in his breath as the damp crown met his hands. ‘‘It’s out!’’

Just the head? Where was the rest of her baby?

"Isn't...it supposed to...be attached...to something?"

She was delirious, he thought. That made two of them. "We need shoulders, Sherry."

The task before her seemed insurmountable. "Aren't you...going to...do...anything?"

Something was wrong. The baby's color didn't look right. There was no time to waste. "Push, Sherry, push." His hand beneath the small head, he looked at her, not wanting to alarm her, wanting her to cooperate. "You're almost there."

At this point all she wanted to do was die in peace. Gulping in air, Sherry shut her eyes tight and concentrated as she gave up the last of herself and pushed. The push ended in a guttural scream.

With the shoulders now out, he tugged the infant out as gently and quickly as he could. "And we have a winner."

"What...what...?"

Turning the baby over on his palm, Sin-Jin was amazed at how tiny the infant was. He patted the baby's back, doing his best to expel any amniotic fluid from the child's nose, mouth and lungs.

"It's a boy."

What was going on? What was he doing? She strained to hear the sound of a baby crying, mewling, something. But there was nothing. "I don't hear..."

The baby had stopped breathing altogether. Quickly Sin-Jin opened the tiny mouth to see if there was anything inside obstructing it. The airway appeared to be clear. But the small chest remained still. Trying to remember everything he'd learned in one year of premed, Sin-Jin placed the baby on his back and gently blew into the tiny mouth before working on the baby's chest.

A panic far greater than the one she'd experienced while in labor was beginning to overtake Sherry. Something was very wrong.

"What is it?" she demanded. "What's wrong with my baby?"

Sherry tried to prop herself up on her elbows and found there wasn't a shred of energy left. She'd used it all giving birth to her baby. The umbilical cord still connected them.

She could almost feel life ebbing away.

"Please," she cried.

The single word said it all. She was pleading with him to save her baby. As if he wouldn't if she hadn't made the entreaty.

He ignored her question, her very presence. All his energy was now focused on bringing air back into the small life he'd helped to bring into the world. Several times he'd pushed on the small chest and then breathed into the tiny mouth.

After what seemed liked an eternity, he felt the smallest of heartbeats beneath his fingertips. Elated, drained, only then did Sin-Jin look up at the baby's mother.

The look in his eyes terrified her. She shouldn't have come up here. She should have stayed home, safe. If she hadn't been so hell-bent on getting this story, her contractions would have overtaken her in her own house, less than five miles away from the hospital. Maybe they wouldn't have come at all. Maybe it was walking uphill that had done it.

Irrational thoughts attacked her from all directions. Had she killed her baby?

Tears gathered in her eyes. "Is he—?"

Sin-Jin was afraid to take his eyes off the infant, afraid that if he did, even for a moment, the baby would stop breathing again.

"He's alive, but he needs to get to a hospital right away."

He couldn't afford to wait.

Moving quickly, Sin-Jin severed the tie between mother and child with a kitchen knife and clamped the end of the cord with a large metal paper clip he'd thought to sterilize.

He wrapped the baby in a towel, amazed at how it seemed to dwarf him, and tucked the infant into her arms.

"I'm going to fly you to Blair Memorial," he told her. It was the closest hospital he knew of that had a neonatal section. He looked at Sherry. The placenta had been expelled, but he wasn't sure if she'd stopped bleeding. The best thing for her would be rest, not to be jostled and then flown a hundred and ten miles, but it couldn't be helped. "This isn't going to be easy," he warned her.

All that mattered was saving her son. "Don't worry about me." Emotion and exhaustion mingled in her voice.

Stooping beside her, Sin-Jin did his best to cover her and slip the parka around her shoulders before he began to pick her up.

With her free hand, she gripped his arm. "That's all right," she told him, "I can walk. Just help me up."

There was no question in his mind that if she tried to gain her feet, she'd pass out again. "The hell you can."

Without another word he rose holding Sherry in his arms as she held the baby to her.

The man was going to pull something, she thought. "We're too heavy for you," she protested weakly.

He steadied himself, then began to cross to the door. "I picked you up when you fainted. The baby was inside of you then. It's just a matter of repositioning." Shouldering open the door, he spared her a look, his expression reproving. "You have got to be the most argumentative woman I've ever encountered."

She felt strength draining from her. It was all she could do to keep her arms around her son.

Live, please live.

"Sorry to hear that."

Greta began to follow him. He paused only long enough to fix the animal with a look. "You stay here and guard the place better than you have been."

The tone of her master's voice had Greta obediently retreating.

"Good dog." Sin-Jin managed to push the door closed with his elbow. Getting a better grip on his cargo, he began walking away from the cabin.

Every step jostled her, underscoring the pain that was running rampant through her body. Her heart was pounding wildly, and she struggled to keep from passing out again. "Adair?"

He kept his eyes fixed on his target, the helicopter

on the landing pad. He cursed the fact that he hadn't had the pad built closer to the cabin.

"What?"

No words seemed good enough. She went with the simplest and hoped that Adair would understand. "Thank you."

He didn't look at her. "You didn't leave me much choice."

Despite his hectic schedule, he'd always made time for exercising and keeping fit. Even so, the hundred yards to the landing pad felt as if it was ten times that as he walked with the woman and child in his arms.

When he finally reached the helicopter, he breathed a silent sigh of relief. Very carefully he eased Sherry into the passenger seat, then strapped her in. Under perfect conditions he would have had a way to secure the baby, as well. But under perfect conditions he wouldn't have had to airlift the infant to the hospital in the first place.

Rounding the front of the helicopter, he got in on the pilot's side. "Hold on, we'll be there in fifteen minutes," he promised.

As he started the engine up, Sin-Jin radioed in his flight plan, and explained his dilemma as well.

Sherry tried to listen, but the sound of the propeller drowned out Adair's voice. Everything was swallowed up by a sea of noise.

She clutched her baby to her, looking down at him to assure herself that he was still breathing, still alive. It all felt surreal, Sherry thought. The delivery, this emergency flight, the pain she was feeling. Even the tall, dark, grim-looking man beside her—all of it surreal. There were tears in her eyes as she looked down at her son. He looked so small, so helpless.

She closed her eyes, the tears seeping through her lashes. *Please let him live,* she prayed. *You don't need another angel, but I do. Please let him stay with me. Please.*

Sherry turned to look at the man piloting the helicopter. In the space of an hour she'd shared an experience with him that had brought her closer to the man than she'd been to almost anyone else.

Who was he, really, and where did she go to find the answers?

There was an emergency crew waiting on the roof of Blair Memorial Hospital. Sin-Jin could see them as he approached the tower building. They stood clustered around a gurney and a glass bassinet, waiting for him to land. The instant the helicopter touched down, they rushed forward with the gurney and the bassinet.

"I thought you'd be a paramedic," the attending physician said, raising his voice to be heard above the din made by the helicopter blades as they came to a slow halt.

Remaining in the 'copter, Sin-Jin helped to guide Sherry and her baby out, gently easing them from their seat.

Sin-Jin shook his head. "Just a civilian. I got them here as fast as I could." Capable hands laid Sherry on the gurney. He saw the look of concern as her son was taken from her and placed in the bassinet. "The baby's less than an hour old. He stopped breathing right after he was born."

"How long?"

Sin-Jin got out from his side and rounded to the gurney. He anticipated the question. ''A minute, maybe less.''

The doctor nodded, then signaled his team to retreat into the building. Gurney and bassinet began to move. ''Thanks, we'll take it from here.''

It was his cue to leave. Sin-Jin had every intention of turning back to his helicopter and just taking off. With any luck he could salvage the rest of his weekend before he had to get back.

But as he started toward the helicopter, his line of vision crossed Sherry's. The look in her eyes spoke volumes. He hesitated a split second. Then, as the team hurried back to the roof's entrance, Sin-Jin found himself following in their wake.

The moment they were back inside the building, the nurse pushing the bassinet looked at him. ''Are you the husband?''

He laughed dryly. No, thank God. ''No, just some guy in the right place at the right time.''

The elevator arrived. The team with its gurney and bassinet filled the interior almost to capacity. The doctor pushed for the fifth floor. ''Lucky for the baby,'' he commented.

''Yeah,'' Sin-Jin murmured in response, ''lucky.'' He saw Sherry lift her hand, groping for his. He took it, wrapping his fingers around hers. He raised an inquisitive brow.

''Did I say thank you?'' she whispered.

Sin-Jin nodded. ''Yes, you did.''

Her eyes held his for a long moment, the sounds around them fading, becoming just so much background noise. ''It wasn't enough.''

The doors sprang open and suddenly they were mobile again. Sherry's fingers remained wrapped around his. Sin-Jin was forced to accompany her as her gurney was hurried down the corridor.

And then the team broke ranks. A nurse and an orderly were guiding the bassinet in another direction. "My baby, where are they taking my baby?" Sherry cried.

The doctor leaned over her gurney. "He's being taken to the neonatal division." His voice was soothing, reassuring. "Don't worry, he'll be well taken care of." Issuing orders regarding the nature of Sherry's immediate treatment, the doctor turned toward Sin-Jin. "If you want to hang around, you can visit with her once we've checked her over and gotten her to a room."

He'd already come farther than he should have. Sin-Jin began to back away. "That's all right, I just wanted to make sure she and the baby were taken care of."

The doctor looked unconvinced. "You're sure?"

"Oh, I'm sure."

Turning on his heel, he walked directly into a nurse. Startled, the woman backed up. Her mouth dropped open and then he saw it, that look of recognition he'd come to dread.

"Aren't you…?"

"No," he said curtly, hurrying past her toward the public elevators before the woman had a chance to ask another question.

As he turned down the corridor, he saw a cluster of reporters and camera crews camped not too far from one of the birthing rooms. He ducked his head down, but not before he'd accidentally made eye contact with one of the cameramen.

Adair. Rusty recognized him instantly. What the hell was he doing here? The man was supposed to be off at a mountain retreat. He'd sent Sherry there.

Concerned, Rusty peered after the man. It was Adair, he was sure of it. He'd been sitting here, cooling his heels for the better part of three hours, waiting for Jennifer Allen, last year's Oscar winner and this year's latest mom-to-be, to give birth. He'd been called down by the station manager and told to join Sherry's anchor replacement, a woman with air pockets for brains. Along with her fellow reporters, he and Lisa Willows were waiting to break the story for the benefit of a Hollywood-enthralled public in need of its latest celebrity fix.

If Adair was here, had he sent Sherry off on a wild-goose chase? Rusty turned and handed a dumbfounded Lisa his camera. "I'll be right back."

"Where are you going?" Lisa called after him.

"Men's room," he tossed over his shoulder. He figured that would do as an excuse.

Rusty turned the corner to where the elevators were located just as Adair got inside. "Wait up," he called.

Sin-Jin had no intentions of doing any such thing. Instead he pressed the button that closed the doors. The last thing he saw was the cameraman racing toward him.

Just his luck, Sin-Jin thought, annoyed. He would have to stumble across a nest of reporters just as he flew a new mother and her baby in. Apparently no good deed went unpunished.

As he rode up in the elevator, he wondered how long he had before some kind of trumped-up story would break. He was certain the reporters would get wind of his being here. He'd had to identify himself when he asked to land on the roof. It was only a matter of time before someone found out about the emergency flight and the baby who had necessitated it.

They'd probably think that the baby was his.

Great. He was going to suffer slings and arrows without ever having even held the woman's hand.

Well, not quite, he amended as he got out on the roof and remembered the way Sherry had looked at him. She'd clutched at his hand and he'd held hers. But that in no way balanced out what he felt certain was going to come his way. He'd had his share of media circuses.

Getting into the helicopter, Sin-Jin started the engine and then cleared the landing pad. He still had part of today and tomorrow before him to try to forget about the rest of the world. That included an overly intrusive news reporter.

Somehow he didn't think he was going to have much luck, but damned if he wasn't going to try.

Chapter Six

"What do you think you're doing having the baby without me?"

Her eyes felt as if they were each weighted down with two fifty-pound plates. With supreme effort, Sherry fought off the drugging effects of well-earned sleep and roused herself as the familiar voice pushed itself into her consciousness.

Surfacing was not easy when every single bone in her body screamed for oblivion or, at the very least, sleep.

When she finally managed to open her eyes, she saw Rusty standing over her, his thin face looking far more drawn and concerned than she recalled seeing in a long time.

Sherry filled her lungs with air before offering a response. "Couldn't be helped." Her reporter's mind kicked in belatedly. Why had he come? Had someone called him? "How did you know I was here?"

As far as she knew, no one knew she was at Blair yet. She hadn't even had the energy to call either of her parents, or Owen. She'd planned to do that after her nap.

"I'm here with Lisa Willows, staking out Jennifer Allen." Rusty nodded toward the door in the general direction of the media circus he'd left behind. "She went into labor early this morning."

This morning. That was when she'd gone into labor. Or was that a hundred years ago?

"Small world." The statement came as a sigh.

"I'll say." Ordinarily not a demonstrative man, Rusty took her hand gently in his. He looked at her with concern. "I looked up and saw Adair walking down the hall. I got this feeling in my gut." Rusty shook his head. "More like a sick feeling, actually, because I knew you'd gone to that cabin retreat to get a lead on him... Are you all right, Sherry?"

It was the same tone he'd used when he'd found out about her quitting the TV station. This time, she didn't have to force a smile to her lips. "I'm fine, achy but fine."

"What happened?"

"I cornered him and went into labor." She laughed at the sound of that.

"But everything turned out okay." He looked at her flattened stomach. "I guess you got here in time."

The words were hard to push out, but she wanted Rusty to know. Someone should know that Adair wasn't the ogre people thought he was. "No, actually, Adair delivered my baby."

Very few things surprised Rusty, but this seemed to qualify. His mouth dropped open as he stared at her. "You're kidding. Darth Vader, the corporate raider, delivered your baby?"

She smiled. "Yes."

He peered at her face. "You're sure you're not just hallucinating? They give you these drugs sometimes—"

"No, I'm not hallucinating." The last few hours were a blur now, dotted with hazy, touching moments and covered in pain. "Adair was very competent—and gentle—from what I remember."

"How did you manage to get here? Medevac?"

"More like Adair-evac." She laughed at the look on Rusty's face and immediately regretted it. There were parts of her body that didn't welcome any kind of exertion no matter how minor. "Adair flew the baby and me here in his helicopter. I didn't realize that Blair had a helicopter landing pad."

"This sounds like one of those improbable movies."

Sherry felt her existing energy ebbing away. "It does, doesn't it?"

"Hell of an angle you got on your story, kid." He spaced his hands in the air, framing a headline. "'St. John Adair delivered my baby.'" Glancing toward Sherry, he saw her shiver. He dropped his hands, immediately solicitous. "What's wrong? Want me to get you a blanket, ring for the nurse, what?"

She groped for his hand, stopping him before he could race off. "No, I'm all right, Rusty. It's just when you put it that way, it sounds like something the tabloids would run.''

''You've got a hell of a lot more finesse than a tabloid,'' Rusty assured her. ''You'll find the right way to phrase it.''

''Yes.''

But even as she said it, Sherry could feel a small glimmer of doubt nudging its way forward. Adair had done something good for her, could she pay him back by doing the one thing he dreaded? Exposing his actions to the scrutiny of the general public.

Damn it, wasn't that why she went up there in the first place? And this was a good thing, it would negate his image as a cold-blooded predator. Or at the very least temper it.

The momentary mental debate tired her even more. There was time for a decision later. Right now, there were more urgent things to tend to than securing her byline in a new area.

She pressed the button on the side railing, and the upper portion of her bed rose.

''Don't tell anyone, Rusty.''

''Hey, it's your exclusive, kid. As far as I'm concerned, I'm just visiting a friend.''

She smiled her gratitude. ''Do me one more favor.''

''You caught me in a generous mood. What?''

She indicated the telephone that was just out of reach on the nightstand. ''Bring the phone over closer, will you? I need to call my parents to let them know they've just entered the grand stage.''

He placed the telephone on the table beside her. ''Your mother's going to love that,'' he quipped.

She grinned. "Mom's still looking for a title that won't make her feel old."

"How about 'Your Highness'?"

"Not warm enough." Sherry began dialing. "Have you seen him yet? My son," she added. *My son.* How incredible that sounded.

"I'll do that now. Be back in a little while," Rusty promised.

Sherry nodded in response, waving goodbye as she heard the receiver on the other end being picked up. "Hi, Mom. Guess what?"

She'd left her purse.

The shapeless black leather shoulder bag was now sitting on the coffee table, silently mocking him, reminding him that he had unfinished business.

Sin-Jin hadn't seen the purse when he'd walked back into the cabin that afternoon. It probably would have remained on the floor under the table if it hadn't been for Greta. The setter had drawn his attention to it by barking at the bag as if it was some kind of dark interloper.

Stretched out on the sofa, about to finally dig into Tom Clancy's latest action thriller, he'd told the dog to be quiet. Greta had responded by placing the bag at his feet.

Looking at the offending item now, he frowned. He'd intended to have no further contact with Sherry Campbell. Now he had her purse, which necessitated interaction of some sort, even if just through a courier. He wasn't about to entrust something as important as a purse to the postal service.

For just a moment he considered looking through

the purse. After all, she'd invaded his privacy. He would be within his rights invading hers. Turnabout was only fair play.

He left the purse where it was.

Fair play or not, by rifling through it he'd be sacrificing his principles, giving in to the curiosity that unexpectedly spiked through him.

So far the woman had managed to invade his life and come perilously close to sabotaging his principles.

"Looks like we're not rid of her yet, eh, Greta?"

The Irish setter barked. He could have sworn there was a sympathetic note in the sound and that she was agreeing with him.

With a resigned sigh, Sin-Jin abandoned Tom Clancy and rose to his feet, feeling too restless to settle in and give the book its due. He needed to move, to clear his brain.

"C'mon, girl, let's go for a walk." He took her red leash down from the hook where he kept it when they visited the cabin. "But if you flush out any more reporters, you're going straight to the pound where I found you." Greta wagged her tail in response, fairly hopping from paw to paw, nothing short of unlimited adoration in her big brown eyes. Sin-Jin wasn't taken in for a moment. "Don't give me that smug look," he warned.

Looping her leash over her head and securing it, he walked out the door. It was going to be a long walk.

Sherry braced her hand against the railing to steady herself and give support to knees that still insisted on being wobbly. She was in the hospital corridor, looking in through the large bay window. The neonatal ICU was located just down the hall from the regular nursery, where all the babies who didn't have problems were safely nestled—on display for doting parents, relatives and friends to come by and view them.

Here, the population was greatly reduced. There were only ten incubators in the neonatal intensive care unit. Ten little souls were born tinier than the rest, but just as mighty, just as pure.

She leaned her forehead against the glass, telling herself everything was going to be all right. She forced back tears so she could see him more clearly. Her son's incubator was positioned second from the left. Tiny baby girls buffered him on both sides. She prayed for all of them.

This was the third time she'd made the pilgrimage today. Three times so that she could assure herself that all was well. That her son was well. Because he was hooked up to a machine that monitored his vital signs, he couldn't be brought to her, but she could come to visit him all she wanted.

Earlier today she'd actually held him for a few minutes. She'd sat down in a rocking chair while a young nurse had carefully placed her baby in her arms. His weight hardly registered. The lump in her throat felt heavier.

She had bags of sugar in her pantry that weighed more.

Holding him had been almost too much for her. Giving him back to the nurse had been harder.

He looked so tiny, she thought, lying there, one

tube monitoring every breath he took, every function of his body, another allowing him to get the nourishment he needed. She should be the one nourishing him, not some tube. It hurt her heart just to look at him.

It was all her fault.

"You shouldn't blame yourself."

The deep voice startled her. It was as if it had somehow delved into her mind, into her heart.

She placed it instantly, before she even turned around.

Adair.

The very last person in the world she would have expected. With effort, still bracing herself on the railing, she managed to half turn her body toward him. The casual look was gone. He was back in uniform again: an expensive designer suit, complete with a shirt and tie, the cost of which would probably feed a family of six for a month.

"What makes you think I blame myself?"

He'd seen it in her eyes, reflected in the ICU glass as he came up behind her. "I didn't get to where I am today by not being able to read body language."

At another time she might have made an attempt to protest, but it was taking all the energy she had just to stand here. Besides, he was right. She did feel guilty. "If I hadn't gone up there after you—"

He'd never had much patience with second-guessing a situation. And hindsight was only good if it taught you something about the future, not the past. "He still might have arrived early. You didn't exactly play half-court basketball that day."

''Maybe not, but I did walk up the side of a mountain.''

''Half a mile,'' Sin-Jin pointed out. He'd located her car after he'd returned. She hadn't lied, the car wouldn't start. The battery had been a faulty one. He'd had the local mechanic put in a new one, then hired the man's two sons to bring the car back into the city. ''And you walked, you didn't hop.''

That he was actually trying to make her feel better stunned her. Was this the same man who'd ruthlessly gone in and closed down a chain of discount department stores that had been around for the past fifty-one years? ''Still, I can't help thinking—''

''What-ifs only make you doubt yourself the next time you have a decision to make,'' he informed her gruffly. ''Don't waste your time on them.''

''Is that the secret of your success?''

''Let's keep this friendly,'' he advised. ''No questions.''

For the time being, she retreated. Adair had delivered her son. She owed him. But there was one thing she did want to know. ''Not even to ask what you're doing here?''

''I could say I was stalking you to give you a taste of your own medicine—''

Her eyes met his and she experienced a little shiver that took her utterly by surprise.

''Being stalked by a rich, handsome man, I think I can handle that.'' She turned completely away from the ICU window, intending on walking back to her room, but the simple motion made her light-headed. Afraid of passing out, she grabbed for his arm, her fingers digging in before she realized what she was doing. Sherry flushed, "Sorry, every time I'm around you, I seem to get light-headed."

What little color she'd had in her cheeks was draining away. "Maybe I should get you into bed," he said.

That sounded like a very good idea, but she felt the need to cover her weakness with a quip. "Why, Mr. Adair, I bet you say that to all the women you meet."

"Only the ones in fuzzy blue slippers," he deadpanned. The expression on his face was dubious. "Can you walk?"

"I can walk," she assured him with less than unwavering confidence. One tentative step later had her hesitating. "Maybe if I just held on to your arm—for good luck."

"Nobody's ever said that to me before." Sin-Jin presented his arm to her, waiting. She hooked her arm through it, trying hard not to lean on him too much. They began to walk down the hallway very slowly. "So what are you doing here, besides providing escort service to wobbly newly minted mothers?"

"I brought your purse." She looked at him quizzically. With everything that had happened, she'd forgotten all about that. "You left it in the cabin. And," he slipped his free hand into his pocket and pulled out a set of keys, "to give you this."

She looked at them, lightning striking her brain and activating it. "Car keys. Oh God, the car—"

She looked so worried he was quick to set her at ease. "You were right, there was something wrong with it. I had it fixed and then had someone drive it down to your place."

Her place. She stopped taking baby steps and looked at him. "You know where I live?"

"I know everything."

She resumed walking. The man was coming across like a regular Renaissance man. "Delivering babies, flying helicopters, fixing cars, detective. I'm beginning to believe that you do."

He didn't want her making too much of it. It was all just common sense. "I believe in being prepared for all contingencies."

"Apparently." She stopped before the door marked 512. "This is my room."

His mouth curved in a half smile. "Yes, I know."

"Sorry, I forgot for a minute." She leaned against it rather than turn the door latch. The door gave, opening. "You know everything."

The quip died on her lips as she walked into the room. There was a large, cut-glass vase on her table, filled with a dozen of the reddest long-stem roses she'd ever seen. There were flowers in her room, several arrangements from family and friends. Even Owen had sent a basket. But nothing like this.

The roses took her breath away. "Did I forget those at your cabin, too?"

He regarded her guardedly. Was that just a slip, or was she baiting him? "It's not my cabin, it belongs to John Fletcher and no, you didn't. I don't like showing up empty-handed when I go somewhere."

"You brought the purse," she reminded him, tongue in cheek. She noticed something else just behind the vase. "And a football." Sherry looked at him. "I'm afraid you're going to have to wait a few days before I'm up to playing."

He brought her to the edge of her bed. She sank down gratefully. "It's for your son."

Yesterday came back to her, at least a fragment of it did. "That's right, the football metaphor. You being the wide receiver." She beamed, proud of herself for remembering.

"I wasn't sure you heard that."

"I heard everything, I just couldn't assimilate it all until later." Sitting down now, she felt almost human again.

"As I recall, you were a little indisposed at the time." He watched her toe off her slippers one at a time.

"Just a little," she agreed. And then she turned somber. What she couldn't remember was whether or not she'd expressed her gratitude. "Look, I don't know how to thank you. Nothing seems good enough."

He hadn't done it for the thanks, she'd been in need of help. He would have done the same for Greta. Faster, probably. But if she was really serious, he had a way for her to express her gratitude. "I think something will occur to you."

He was talking about the story, she thought. She really wasn't at liberty to tell him that she wouldn't pursue the story, that, if anything, his actions had aroused her curiosity. She wanted to know more about the man who was a ruthless businessman by day and a rescuing Renaissance man by night.

"What does occur to me right now is that you

have got to be possibly the most well-rounded person I have ever met."

Flattery turned him off. He'd suffered too much of being pandered to by people who were stupid enough to believe that flattery made a difference in the way he viewed things, or them.

"Like I said, I like being prepared."

"There's prepared and then there's *prepared.*" She studied him in silence for a moment. "Is there anything you can't do?"

He looked her in the eye. "I can't seem to get you to stop asking questions."

He didn't look annoyed, she thought. Progress. "Occupational hazard."

She still looked pale, he thought. "How are you feeling?"

She thought of her sore bottom. Stretching was definitely out. "Well, I don't think I'll be doing any intricate yoga positions for a couple of weeks, but all things considered, I'm doing great." Her smile deepened as she looked up at him. "If you hadn't been there for us—"

He shrugged off her words before she could finish. "Someone else would have."

He was really sincere about that, she realized. One of the richest men in the country resisted compliments and gratitude. Amazing. "I guess I should add modesty to that list."

That did make him laugh, however briefly. "There'd be a lot of people who'd dispute that with you."

She liked the sound of his laugh. Deep, rich, like the first coffee in the morning. "They'd be wrong."

He rubbed his chin, regarding her. She didn't seem the pandering sort. "I don't give way before flattery, Ms. Campbell."

"And I'm not trying to flatter, Mr. Adair." Her expression softened. "I think after everything we've been through, we don't need to be that formal."

It was time for him to leave, he decided. He'd already been here too long. He'd only meant to leave her purse and the gifts. Discovering the room empty should have been a godsend. But something had urged him on to see how the baby was doing, and then he'd found himself compelled to comment once he'd seen the reflection of her face in the glass.

"Yes, we do. Well, now that you have your purse and your keys—"

She smiled, nodding at the vase. "And my roses."

"And your roses," he allowed, already withdrawing, "I'd better go."

Suddenly she didn't want him to leave. Not because he was her story, but because he was the man who'd come to her aid. Whether he liked it or not they'd bonded, up in that cabin.

"You could stay. We could talk. Off the record," she added for good measure.

Sin-Jin looked at her pointedly. "This has *all* been off the record," he informed her. "And I have a meeting to get to."

Still on the edge of the bed, she tried to scoot back and wasn't very successful at it. And then, before she knew it, Adair had placed his hands on her waist and moved her back. Before she could say anything, he threw the blanket over her legs, covering her.

"What are you smiling about?" he asked.

She wiggled out of her robe. Aware that her night-gown was slipping from her shoulder, she pulled the strap back up. "I was just thinking that you're not nearly the coldhearted man you want the general public to think you are."

He felt something stir in his gut as he looked at her. "I don't care what anyone thinks, Ms. Campbell. And I am a coldhearted man. The general public is right."

She inclined her head, knowing better but too tired to argue. "Have it your way."

"I generally do, Ms. Campbell, I generally do. You'll forgive me if I don't say, 'See you around.'"

"You don't have to say it," she told him as he began to leave. "Some things are a given."

She had the pleasure of seeing him stop for a fraction of a second before continuing on his way out. For that fraction of a second she knew she'd gotten to him. Which was only fair. Because the feeling was mutual.

Chapter Seven

"What do you mean, 'The bill's already been taken care of'?"

Sherry wasn't in the mood to untangle someone else's bureaucratic mistakes. After a three-day stay at the hospital, she was finally going home. Going home without her baby. The infant was still not ready to leave the shelter of the incubator and monitors that watched over him. Sherry was having a great deal of trouble coming to terms with that.

Standing beside the wheelchair that hospital regulations dictated she use to make her exit, and buffered on either side by her parents, Sherry looked at the older woman at the cashier's desk.

The woman smiled at her brightly. "Just that, it's been taken care of."

Had she missed something? Sherry tried to remember. No, there was some mistake. "But that's not possible. I haven't even given you my insurance card." She held it aloft for the woman's benefit.

In the confusion of her emergency entrance, she'd just assumed that no one had thought to take her insurance information. It seemed rather odd to her, given what hospital expenses were these days, but she wanted to rectify the situation before she was discharged.

But when she'd stopped the nurse pushing her wheelchair from taking her outside so that she could provide the necessary information, the billing clerk had politely but firmly refused to take it down because apparently there was no need.

Connor Campbell gently edged his daughter aside as he leaned over the desk. A short bull of a man with a thick mane of white hair, he had a presence that immediately gave him center stage. He smiled encouragingly at the clerk.

"There must be some mistake. Maybe you have my daughter mixed up with another Campbell. It's a common enough name."

With a patient smile the woman retreated to her computer and reentered Sherry's information. The same screen came up a second time. She shook her head and raised her eyes to Connor. "Nope, says right here, 'Paid in full.'"

Connor frowned. "Never heard of an insurance company being eager to pay out on a claim, especially before the claim's been made."

The woman looked up at him brightly. "Payment didn't come from an insurance company." She looked back at the screen to double-check before she continued. ''It's a voucher from Adair Industries.''

Sherry's mouth dropped open. ''What?''

Without waiting for an invitation, Sherry pushed aside the wheelchair and came around to the other side of the woman's desk to look at the screen herself.

Stunned, the clerk began to protest. ''Ma'am, you can't just—''

Sherry was in no mood for opposition. ''Yes, I can 'just' when it concerns my bill.'' Amazed, vaguely annoyed, she read the notation on the screen. The woman had been right. ''Son of a gun,'' she whispered, stunned. The payment was coming from Adair Industries all right. Which meant the money was somehow coming from Adair.

Why?

Connor raised a bemused, shaggy eyebrow as he fixed his daughter with a quizzical look. ''Just what kind of secrets did you promise to bury for this man?''

Her head jerked up. She knew her father was kidding, but deception of any kind was a sore point for her. Drew had deceived her when he'd made her believe that he loved her, that there were no other women in his life. Instead the man was probably just one female short of a harem.

''None,'' she told him tersely. ''I didn't promise to bury any secrets.'' And then, because it was her father, her voice softened. ''He never told me any secrets.''

No man was prouder of his daughter than Connor Campbell. He'd stake his reputation on her honor.

Connor exchanged glances with his wife as if to wonder if there was something going on between Sherry and this man?

"Then why's he being so generous?" Connor asked.

Sherry sighed, shoulders rising and falling in a helpless shrug. "I don't know."

Her mother had what to her was a plausible explanation. "Could be the man's just got a good heart. Well, it's possible," she insisted when both her daughter and her husband looked at her as if she'd suddenly lost her mind.

Connor pressed his lips together as he shook his head. "Oh, Sheila, if you only read the paper once in a while instead of using it to wrap things with, you'd know the man's a cold devil."

The petite, trim woman remained undaunted. "Even the devil's got some good in him if you look hard enough."

To which Connor shook his head. "Incorrigible. You'd think after being on this earth for—" his wife shot him a warning look "—twenty-nine plus years," he said carefully, "she'd know that the world isn't a big sunny garden."

The soft Irish lilt in Sheila's voice became more pronounced whenever she grew adamant. "You only see the dark side, Connor, my love. I choose to see the light. I think of the two of us, I'm the happier one."

Sherry frowned. "Well, I don't care what color St. John Adair sees, there's no way I'm going to let him pay my bills for me." Coming around to the other side of the desk again, she slid her insurance card across the counter toward the woman. ''Here, contact my insurance company for actual payment of the account.''

The woman shook her head. ''The hospital will only wind up sending it on to you.'' The woman gently pushed the card back to Sherry. ''We can't collect twice on the same account.''

Temporarily stymied, Sherry refused to give up entirely. ''But you'll need the information for my son's bill. He's still in the neonatal section.''

The woman typed in ''Campbell, Infant,'' then looked up at Sherry. She hesitated slightly before saying, ''It seems that bill's covered, too.''

That really didn't make any sense. ''But the charges are still coming in.'' The doctors had told her that her son was going to have to remain here at least a week, if not two.

The woman took a deep breath, then launched into the explanation. ''There's a voucher attached to the account. All expenses will be paid by—''

Sherry closed her eyes as she echoed the clerk's next words. ''Adair Industries.''

Connor snorted, then slipped his arm around his daughter. ''Maybe helping you deliver the baby was like a religious experience for him,'' he offered. When she looked at him, Connor punctuated his guess with a wide shrug.

Sherry didn't know what to say, what to make of it. This act of so-called generosity was entirely against type. Although now that she thought about it, she really didn't know what ''type'' Adair was. She had only hearsay to act on, and that wasn't very satisfying. Up close and personal, the man certainly didn't fit into any mold that she knew of. It wasn't as if he was fearful of the press or exposure, he just didn't like the media. Not all that unusual, really.

There had to be a catch, but what?

Behind her the nurse who had volunteered to usher her out shifted. She was still holding on to the wheelchair. "I need to get back to my floor," she prodded gently. "Could we get you to your dad's car?"

Relieved that the discussion was tabled for the time being, Connor responded quickly.

"Sure thing." He patted Sherry's hand. "We'll get to the bottom of this, don't you worry, but first things first. I'll bring it round to the entrance," he told the nurse, then turned to his wife. "Coming, Grandma?"

Sheila Mckinney Campbell drew herself up to her full five feet, squaring her shoulders defiantly as she fixed her husband with a dark look. "I'll wait right here with Sherry, and I'll thank you not to call me that, Connor."

Connor only laughed as he hurried off to fetch his vehicle.

Sherry sighed, pocketing her insurance card. There was nothing more to be done here today. Bracing her hands on both armrests, she sank down in the wheelchair again and allowed herself to be taken down the long corridor.

"You know he's just doing it to get to you, Mom." She tried not to notice the baby items that were displayed in the window as they passed the gift shop.

"I know that." Sheila patted her daughter's hand as she walked alongside the wheelchair. "I love the baby, I truly do. It's just that I don't think I'm quite ready to be called—'' she took a deep breath ''—that name yet.''

Sherry glanced at her mother. With her flawless Irish skin and her red hair that still required no assistance from any chemical product on the market, Sheila Campbell looked more like her older sister than her mother. She could understand her mother's ambivalent feelings.

''Work something out soon, Mom. I don't want him growing up saying 'hey you' every time he wants your attention.''

Sheila nodded, her red hair bobbing about her face in lively waves. ''Let me think about it a little more,'' she murmured.

Sherry barely heard her. Her mind was elsewhere. Like a dog with a bone, she was trying to break it down into manageable pieces. Why was Adair doing this? What was in it for him?

The puzzle helped to keep her mind off the fact that she was leaving her son behind.

''He's doing very well.'' Moving softly, the evening shift nurse came up and stood behind her as Sherry sat with her baby, rocking in a chair the hospital provided. ''If he keeps on this way, you'll be able to take him home in another week.''

Another week. It felt as if an eternity had already gone by, even though it was only a matter of a few days since she had left the hospital. As she was still unable to drive safely, her parents and friends took turns bringing her to the hospital, where she remained a few hours at a time, bonding with her son.

Praying. Looking forward to the day she could be around him for more than a few revolutions of the hour hand.

"That's good." Sherry bent over and kissed the tiny hand that splayed out over her palm. The baby stirred, filling her heart to maximum capacity.

"I want you home, little one."

"I know. I bet your brother'll be happy to hear that."

Sherry looked up at the woman, confused. She was an only child. "My brother?"

"Yes." The nurse paused to beam down at the infant in his mother's arms. "He's been stopping by here late every night. It's past visiting hours, really," she confided to Sherry, "but he persuaded one of the other nurses to let him in for a few minutes. Wish my brother was that attentive to my kids. I can't get him to even remember their birthdays."

It couldn't be Rusty or Owen because both had told her about their visits. "Are you sure there isn't some mistake? I don't have a brother."

The woman looked at her, surprised and confused. "Tall, quiet, *really* good-looking." A small sigh escaped the nurse.

It had to be Adair. "Does he say why he's here?"

"Well, sure. To see how his nephew's doing. That's what he told Doris," the nurse added, mentioning one of the nurses on the night shift.

For the past few days, Sherry's professional life had taken a back seat to her private one. She was busy trying to return to normal, and spent what time she had visiting her son. But this thing with Adair was turning into a mystery. Maybe it was time to take the reporter in her off hold. ''What time does he come by?''

''Nine,'' the nurse answered. ''Every night like clockwork.''

The woman made it sound as if she made it a point to be in the area, she thought. Well, maybe next time around, Sherry would, too.

Later that same day Sherry gingerly eased herself out of Lori's car. Her bottom still felt a little sore if she sat for more then ten minutes at a time. She couldn't wait to get back to her old self.

Closing the passenger door, she looked at her former Lamaze instructor. ''I really appreciate the lift, Lori.''

Lori was still in the vehicle. She needed to park the car. She'd just stopped at the front entrance to shorten the distance for Sherry.

''Don't thank me, I had to come here, anyway.'' She leaned out the window as Sherry rounded the hood of the car. ''You have someone to pick you up? Because I can double back later after class if you don't.''

Sherry shook her head. ''I'll be fine. I'm going to call my father when I'm finished.''

Lori nodded, taking the car out of park. Her foot still hovered on the brake. ''Come by and join us for ice cream next week. The Mom Squad just isn't the same without you.'' She did a quick calculation. ''You should be able to drive by then.''

Sherry missed seeing the group, especially Chris and Joanna. They and Lori had gotten together and bought her a beautiful hand-carved crib, delivering it to her parents' house the day she'd left the hospital. Her father had transported it to her house today. Her parents were there now, putting it together. If she knew them, they were butting heads as to how it should be done. She was far better off here.

Sherry smiled broadly. "I'd love to."

"Good, see you at the ice-cream parlor." Lori waved, taking off to the parking lot. "I hope they tell you that you can take him home tomorrow," she called out.

Sherry turned away and walked in through Blair's electronic doors. There was no chance of that. The physician who had come by later this afternoon had confirmed the nurse's prognosis. She'd already been by twice today, once when Owen had dropped her off and once with her mother. This time around she wasn't here just to see her son, but her son's "uncle" as well. If Adair actually showed up tonight.

She still had her doubts.

They disappeared when she stepped out on the floor and made her way to the neonatal ward. Approaching the bay window, she saw a tall man standing in the dimmed corridor light.

Adair.

Damn it, this just wasn't making any sense. From everything she'd gleaned about him, he was an incredibly busy man who was forced to schedule every breath he took. What was he doing here?

She echoed the question aloud as she drew closer. "What are you doing here?"

He glanced in her direction as if he'd expected her to show up. Was clairvoyance to be added to his repertoire?

"It's a free country, Ms. Campbell, and I am over the age of eighteen." He turned back to look at the babies in the ward. Babies who were struggling for what everyone else took for granted. Life. "Unless I break the law, I am not accountable for my actions to anyone—" he slanted a look at her again "—not even a woman as lovely as you."

She couldn't say why the compliment didn't bounce off her the way so many others did. Instead, it seemed to find a crack and seep in, warming her when she didn't want to be warmed.

"Maybe not accountable," she allowed, crossing her arms before her, "but a few explanations might be in order."

He had to admit there was something magnificent about her when she tossed her head that way. He was reminded of a painting he'd once seen of St. Joan decked out in full battle regalia, ready to uphold the honor of God and country.

"I—"

She wasn't about to let him veer off the track and he had that look about him. Like a man who was just about to charm the socks off a barefoot woman. Suddenly, she saw what every other woman saw in him. "Like why did you pay my hospital bill?"

He shrugged vaguely, his broad shoulders moving comfortably beneath his navy jacket. "Act of charity."

He'd pressed the wrong button. Her eyes narrowed. "I don't need charity."

"Act of kindness, then." He pinned her with a look, beginning to wonder about the woman who had attempted to beard him in his den, who would risk uncomfortable surroundings just to get what she was after. ''You can't tell me you don't need kindness. I'm of the opinion that most people need kindness.''

The sentiment oddly echoed her mother's. Who would have thought they were of like mind? No one, because they weren't. He was after something; she was sure of it. ''Like you?''

The smile slowly curved his lips. Why hadn't she noticed how sensuous they were before?

''I'm not most people,'' he replied.

She forced her mind back on business. That was what this man was all about, business. ''But you wouldn't be averse to kindness. Perhaps you think that paying my hospital bill and my son's hospital bill will buy me off?''

His expression sobered, wiping away all traces of any smile that might have existed. ''I am not in the habit of explaining myself, just as I'm not in the habit of buying people off.'' Feeling charitable, he shared a little of his business philosophy with her. It had stood him in good stead in his private life, as well. ''People you can buy off are too cheap to want to keep.''

''Very profound,'' she inclined her head. When she raised it again, her eyes pinned him to the window. ''So exactly why did you pay my bill?''

It had been a whim, pure and simple. He had no better explanation for it. But he couldn't afford to let it get around that he was governed by things that weren't grounded in cold, hard reasoning.

''You're my first delivery. I was feeling generous.'' Most women would have let it go at that.

"Don't look a gift horse in the mouth, Ms. Campbell."

She didn't like being dismissed. "The Greeks didn't and it got them in a whole lot of trouble."

The remark made him smile again, almost against his will. "You're not Greek."

"I'm also not naive, Mr. Adair." If she knew nothing else about him, she knew that he didn't do anything without a reason. She wanted to know what it was. "There is no free lunch and you can't get something for nothing. Now what is it that you want?"

No good deed went unpunished, he thought again. Served him right for being impulsive.

"Ideally?" There was a hint of sarcasm in his voice. "Peace in our time." She wanted a reason, all right, he'd give her one, even if it hadn't been the one behind his actions. "If not peace in our time, then no more of this kind of reporting." He took a folded sheet of newspaper out of his pocket and handed it to her.

It wasn't a newspaper, she realized, it was the front page of one of the supermarket tabloids she blocked out whenever she shopped. Her eyes widened as she read the headline: Adair Flies Mistress and Secret Love Child to Hospital.

Mrs. Farley had brought this to his attention. The look in the older woman's eyes had been anger. A similar one was entering Campbell's eyes. You couldn't fake that kind of a response, he judged.

"I see by the look on your face that you didn't leak the story to this rag."

Crumpling the page in her hand, she stared at him.

How dare he even think that? He dared, a small voice whispered, because he didn't know her and because she'd followed him to his haven, invading it. What did she expect?

Sherry struggled to put a lid on her anger. ''I'm a serious journalist, Mr. Adair, not a gossipmonger.''

He found himself wanting to hear her calling him by his first name. The thought had come out of nowhere, and he promptly returned it there.

''Serious journalist,'' he echoed. ''Do serious journalists write about how the Hathaway twins have made good in their transition from child stars to adult sensations?''

He'd read her article? Or just the headline? In either case she didn't see him as the type to even know that section of the newspaper existed.

''They do if they're trying to work their way up into getting a serious byline. My editor gives me an assignment. I do it.'' She saw a hint of a smirk take over his lips. He obviously didn't believe her. ''Besides, if you read the article, all my facts were correct and, unlike you, my subjects weren't hostile.''

She didn't strike him as the obedient type, job or no job. ''They were also young and welcomed publicity.''

She gave him a long, measuring look. He was how old? Thirty-three? He made himself sound years older than that. ''You're not exactly Mr. Wilson—'' She could see what he was thinking. ''And I'm not Dennis the Menace.''

He laughed. The sound wasn't off-putting. ''Matter of opinion, Ms. Campbell, matter of opinion.''

She was getting sidetracked. By his laugh, by his

smile and his manner. She was definitely off her game, but she intended to make a comeback. Now. "I can pay my own bills, Adair. I'm not exactly from the wrong side of the tracks."

He nodded. The mistake had been his. He should have left well enough alone. "No, you're very comfortable, very bright when it comes to investing your money. Admirably frugal, too."

Her eyes widened again. "You had me checked out?"

It took effort not to be mesmerized by the blue orbs. "How does it feel to have the shoe on the other foot? Pinches, doesn't it?"

He was comparing apples and oranges. "I don't merit national attention for doing what I do."

He could beg to differ. She'd been a local celebrity, eased out of her job, he'd discovered, because of her condition. He had to admit he admired her spirit, if not her vocation.

"And I do." It wasn't a question.

"I'm afraid it goes with the territory you've picked out for yourself," Sherry said, relenting, thinking of how kind he'd been to her while she was giving birth. Like it or not, there was a soft spot in her heart because of that. "Why do you want people to think you're this dark-hearted ogre?"

"Because people have a healthy respect for ogres." And kept a decent distance away from them, he added silently.

"That's fear, not respect," she corrected.

He inclined his head. Semantics. "That works for me, too."

"You want people to fear you?"

"I want people to keep out of my private life."

She read between the lines and placed herself in his position. She wouldn't have been able to put up with it. Her world was filled with people. People she cared about. "Must be lonely."

The note of pity in her voice took him by surprise. And offended him. The last time anyone had pitied him was Mrs. Farley. He'd been fourteen years old. "That is for me to know—and you not to find out." He had someplace else to be. "If you'll excuse me, I'm going to call it a night."

There was no hesitation on her part. She recognized opportunity even when it tiptoed in rather than knocked. "Could you drop me off?"

She'd managed to catch him off guard. But just for a moment. "You really do have a hell of a lot of nerve, don't you?"

Her smile was wide. "No argument."

"Finally." And then he sighed. "All right, come on, I'll take you home." Already on his way to the elevator, he slanted a look at her. "And I'd stop smiling smugly if I were you."

"Yes, sir."

There was a grin in her voice a mile wide. Sin-Jin didn't trust himself to comment.

Chapter Eight

He drove fast. It didn't surprise her. A man like Adair—intense, goal oriented—would drive fast. He would do most things fast.

Would he make love fast, too?

The thought sneaked up on her, but she pushed it aside. It wasn't remotely part of her research. She blamed it on the song playing in his CD player and the crumpled tabloid headline in her pocket.

The music wasn't filling up the spaces. On the contrary, the interior of the Mercedes was getting smaller with each mile that passed by.

Sherry cleared her throat. ''I didn't think you listened to music.''

The statement brought the slightest curve to his lips. ''Did you think I listened to all-news stations all the time?''

"Not while you slept."

"Culture has a definite place in the world." He spared her a glance. "It refines people, nurtures their souls."

That sounded incredibly lofty. Sherry ventured a guess. "Lulls them into a state of tranquility so that you can take them over more easily?"

"So my competitors say."

"I didn't think you had competitors."

He slanted another glance in her direction a moment before he merged into the extreme right-hand lane. "Flattery isn't going to get you anywhere."

"Not flattery, observation."

The car ahead of him was moving too slowly; he changed lanes quickly. "More flattery."

"You're a hard man to talk to."

He checked his mirrors, then changed lanes again, moving back into the lane he'd just vacated. "So I've been told."

They were almost there. She didn't remember ever making the trip so quickly. "You're going to need to take the Jeffrey Road off-ramp." It was coming up within a matter of seconds.

He was already easing onto the off-ramp. A red light at the end prevented him from making a smooth transition onto the thoroughfare. "I know where you live, remember?"

She knew he'd sent the vehicle she'd left stranded on the mountain to her address, but she hadn't expected him to actually recall what it was. "With all the things you have to remember? I'm impressed."

He shrugged off the comment. "Don't be. I have a photographic memory."

Another personal tidbit. She wondered if he realized that he was opening up to her, however slightly. She baited him, recalling a recent article she'd read.

"Scientists maintain there's no such thing, that it's simply a matter of teaching yourself how to memorize things."

The light turned green. He pressed the accelerator. The road before him stretched out with a smattering of traffic. "Scientists have been known to be wrong."

"So how does that work, you look at something and zap, it's stuck in your mind forever?"

He had no idea how it worked, only that he could recall anything at will. He used it like a tool. "Something like that."

She shook her head, trying to imagine what that was like. "Must get awfully crowded in there."

He smiled. The woman just didn't give up attempting to coax information out of him. Since it did no harm, he indulged her. "I manage."

"All right." Sherry shifted in her seat to look at him. "Let's see if it works. What's the name of the first girl you ever kissed?"

It was time to stop indulging. "Clever, but no cigar."

They'd reached their destination. He pulled up in front of her house and turned toward her. The streetlight standing before the house next door to hers scattered just enough light into his vehicle to dance along only part of her face, highlighting it. Something stirred within him, nudging curiosity forward.

Getting out of the car, he rounded the hood and

went to the passenger side. He opened the door, taking her hand as she got out.

She found herself standing much too close to the man. Neither of them took a step away.

"I'd rather tell you the name of the next woman I'm going to kiss," he said.

There was something hypnotic about his eyes. "Does she know?"

His smile was slow, drifting under her skin. They both knew what he was saying. "I've got a feeling that she might have a good idea."

Sherry felt her heart accelerating. She became aware that she had stopped breathing, and forced air back into her lungs. "Doesn't that constitute bribery or conflict of interest or something like that?"

Sin-Jin moved her hair away from her shoulder, exposing her neck. "You're the reporter, you tell me."

Her heart was now doing some serious beating. She wondered if he could see it vibrating in her throat. "I suppose it could be seen as research."

"Whose?"

The word skimmed along her skin, teasing her. Tantalizing her. "Mine," she breathed.

His smile broadened. "Whatever works for you."

Sin-Jin dove his fingers into her hair, framing her face with his hands. He paused a fraction of a moment, looking at her.

"Memorizing my face?" she asked, surprised that at this point, she could even form words. Everything within her was holding its breath.

"I don't need to." The next moment, before she could ask why, Sin-Jin brought his lips down to hers.

Sherry wasn't sure just exactly what she was expecting. Maybe disappointment. No one could live up to the buildup she'd just created in her mind.

She didn't find it. Disappointment had left the building on winged feet.

The one thing she hadn't expected was to be affected, not to this extent. She'd bounced back fairly well from her pregnancy in the past couple of days, so she couldn't blame the weakness she felt in her knees on anything remotely postpartum.

She had to put the blame exactly where it belonged. On the lips of the man kissing her.

After Drew had walked out on her, she had been convinced that she would never feel anything, physical or emotional, for a man again. It was far too painful to expose yourself that way, to hand yourself up, naked and wanting, to another human being. She'd closed off all ports of entry to her soul and had thrown away the keys.

Somehow, they'd been found again.

Without thinking it through, Sherry leaned into the kiss. Into Sin-Jin. Savoring the wildfire that was suddenly ignited within her.

She knew to the moment the last time she'd been kissed.

And then she knew nothing at all.

He was a man of reason, given to doing things for definite, concrete reasons that at times made sense only to him. But he wasn't entirely sure just why he was kissing her, or what had brought him to this juncture.

He just knew he had to kiss her.

When it came to Sherry Campbell, fledgling ace

reporter, he wasn't sure of anything, not his actions, not his thoughts. What he was sure of was that he was reacting to her despite all the self-imposed restraints that had been put in place over the years. The fact astonished Sin-Jin.

At a very young age he'd promised himself never to emulate either of his parents. He would never go from mate to mate, investing his soul only to be disappointed. Love, to him, was far too important a thing to tarnish, and so it was kept under wraps, hidden, never to venture out into the light of day. Or the soft, seductive rays of moonlight.

To that end he made himself far too busy to risk entanglements or to waste any time on relationships that were guaranteed an ignoble death by the law of averages he'd observed while growing up.

But there was something about this woman that made him curious, that made him want to put himself at risk. Just a little.

If he pushed aside the circumstances that surrounded their interactions, he'd have to admit that she had stirred him, twisting his gut and waking desire even from the very first.

She tightened her hands on his arms, bracing herself. Her bones were melting, and it wouldn't do to sink down here on her front stoop.

Bells, she was hearing bells. No, wait, that was a cell phone ringing.

Blinking, struggling out of her dazed state, she looked up at Sin-Jin. The words came out in a hoarse whisper. "Is that your phone?"

He found he had to swallow before answering, taking care not to lose his tongue. He wasn't sure exactly what had just happened here, only that it had never happened before.

Sin-Jin cleared his throat. "No, I believe that's yours." Releasing her, he touched his pocket to make sure. "Mine's on vibrate."

Sherry blew out a breath, feeling completely unsteady. Locking her knees rigidly to keep from embarrassing herself, she tossed her hair over her shoulder, praying for nonchalance.

"That's one way to get a thrill. Must be mine, then." Hoping that her hands wouldn't shake, she took out her phone and flipped it open. "Campbell."

"When are you going to call for me to pick you up?"

She closed her eyes and sighed. Saved by the cavalry. Just as well. One more second and she would have permanently forgotten how to breathe.

She dragged her hand through her hair. She saw Sin-Jin looking at her, his dark eyes curious. It took effort to stop the shiver that wanted to shimmy up her spine in its tracks.

"I'm already home, Dad. Just look out the window."

When the light-gray drapes at the front window moved back, she waved. Her father, she mused, looked as if he could be knocked over with a feather.

The next moment the front door was opening. Connor Campbell filled the entry, somehow giving the impression, at five-eight of being larger than life.

"Need any help?"

It wasn't completely clear if her father was addressing the question to her or to the man standing beside her, but Sherry was the one who answered.

"No, we're fine." And then, because it was awkward not to, Sherry began to make introductions. "Dad, this is—"

"St. John Adair, yes, I know," he told Sherry pointedly.

She turned toward Sin-Jin. "Mr. Adair, this is—"

Sin-Jin extended his hand to her father. When the latter grasped it, they shook with the solemnity of two chieftains meeting on the moors. "Connor Campbell, I've read your byline."

Sherry shrugged haplessly. The awkwardness of the moment wouldn't abate. She'd just been kissed by St. John Adair. And she'd kissed him back.

"Well, I'm certainly superfluous here," she murmured to herself.

Sin-Jin dropped his hand to his side as he looked at her. He could still taste her on his lips. "I wouldn't exactly say that."

Connor looked from the tycoon to his daughter. In typical fashion, he made his assessment rapidly. He was rarely wrong.

"Why don't you come in?" He opened the door wider. "The crib's finished—"

"No thanks to your father," Sheila Connor called out, joining them at the door. Sherry was surprised her mother had held out this long. Consuming curiosity was far from an unknown factor in her mother's life. "The least handy man I've ever met." She smiled warmly at the man standing beside Sherry. "He's all thumbs."

Connor wrapped a proprietary arm around his wife's shoulders. She fitted neatly against his side. "Didn't hear you complaining last night."

Sherry made a show of covering her ears as she rolled her eyes. "I don't need to hear this."

"Of course you do, girl," Sheila told her with a laugh that was almost identical to her daughter's. "How else are you going to know that there are good relationships out there and that not all men are like that scum who deserted you?"

The last remark had been for Sin-Jin's benefit, Sherry thought with a sinking feeling inside her. It was a mistake to bring him here, and now she was paying for it.

She wet her lips, feeling oddly nervous. It wasn't a feeling she was accustomed to.

"Sorry about this, Mr.—" She caught herself and could feel a flush creeping up her neck. She prayed that he was farsighted only. "Under the circumstances I guess I'd better call you St. John."

Connor gave the man the once-over. "Huh," he snorted. "Never knew a man to live up to the title of saint." His voice had the ability to be both booming and intimate at the same time, making the listener feel as if he had become an instant friend and been welcomed into Connor's inner circle. "What do your friends call you?"

Sherry looked at him with interest, half expecting the man to say that he had no friends, or, at the very least, that it wasn't any of her father's business *what* they called him.

Instead, he responded, "Sin-Jin."

Connor cracked a wide smile. "Man named after my favorite liquor can't be all bad." He was taking Sin-Jin's arm and ushering him into the house as if it was his to do so, rather than his daughter's. "Come on in a spell, rest your feet—'' he looked at his daughter significantly ''—if not your ears.''

''Sin-Jin has to leave,'' Sherry protested.

Sin-Jin looked at Sherry, wondering if she was aware that she'd slid from Mr. Adair to St. John to Sin-Jin without pause. She'd given him his way out. But he had to admit there was something oddly compelling about the couple who stood before him. About them and the daughter they had produced.

And then the small woman who looked like an older version of her daughter robbed him of his escape. ''Oh, he'll stay for a cup of Irish coffee.'' She looked up at him brightly. ''Won't you, dear?'' Before he could say anything, Sheila had slipped her personality, her Irish lilt and her arm through his and was gently drawing him into the living room.

''I guess I can stay for a few minutes,'' Sin-Jin allowed.

Amused, Sherry watched her mother weave her magic on the man. It occurred to her that had she wanted to, her mother would have made an excellent investigative reporter. It was obvious that Sin-Jin hadn't stood a chance against her.

Maybe her mother could give lessons, she mused, following behind them. She heard her father chuckling beside her and knew he was probably thinking the same thing.

''So that's the mighty St. John Adair, eh?'' Connor commented an hour later as he shut the front door. He turned to look at his daughter. ''Seems rather taken with you, missy. I saw the way he was looking at you.''

Oh, no, she wasn't about to let her father go off on that tangent. Even if he'd seen them kissing, which she was sure he hadn't, there was no basis to believe that Adair had felt anything but curiosity.

"I think you have your looks confused, Dad. He was blaming me for pulling him into all this." She fixed her father with a look. "You can be overwhelming, you know."

Sheila moved to side with her husband, physically as well as verbally. "Say what you will, I like him," she declared.

Connor laughed. "You'd like Satan if he smiled wide enough."

Sheila raised her eyes to his face. "As I recall, my father thought you were the devil incarnate when you first started coming around."

He waved away the story. "Well, we all know your father was always wrong, God-rest-his-soul," he tagged on mechanically.

"Maybe that one time," Sheila acquiesced generously. There was a teasing smile playing on her lips.

Feeling suddenly drained, Sherry decided it was time for her to retreat. She stuck her hands into her pockets, about to say good-night, when her fingers came in contact with a crumpled piece of paper. Drawing it out, she remembered the look on Sin-Jin's face when he handed it to her. His expression had been carefully controlled. This bothered him, she thought.

Impulsively she made up her mind. "Dad, I want you to do me a favor."

Connor looked away from his wife. ''Anything, love.''

She knew how he felt about tabloid journalism. He didn't like to dirty his hands with it. But this was necessary. ''I need a few strings pulled.''

Independent though she'd been since the moment she'd opened her eyes on this world, he'd always made it a point to let her know that he was there, in the background, ready to do anything she needed doing. That's what made them a family. ''You've come to the right man. What is it you need done?''

She took a deep breath. ''Who do you know on the *Bulletin?*''

The shaggy eyebrows drew into a scowling, dismissive line. ''That rag?'' he hooted. ''What makes you think I know someone there?''

''Because you know everyone, dear.'' Sheila patted his chest with the familiarity of a woman who knew her husband's every thought even before it occurred to him. ''Even people who work on that rag. Like William Kelley, remember?'' She turned to Sherry. ''Why are you asking, dear?''

Sherry smoothed out the front page, then held it up for both her parents to see at the same time. She saw anger spring like lightning into her father's eyes. ''I want this to be retracted.''

Sheila took the page from her, reading the headline again in disbelief. She turned to her husband. ''Oh, my God. Connor, you have to make them print an apology. We can't have Sherry's character maligned like this—''

Sherry quickly cut her off. ''It's not my name I'm concerned about, Mother. Sin-Jin saved my son's life and maybe mine, as well.'' She'd begun hemorrhaging shortly after she'd been taken to the hospital. If that had happened while she'd been in the cabin, she might not be having this conversation with her parents now. ''This is not the way to pay him back, especially considering how he feels about his privacy.''

Connor plucked the page from his wife. His scowl deepened and he muttered something under his breath that was best left unheard.

''Consider it done, love. The retraction's going in the day after tomorrow. Sooner if I can get ahold of Blake Andrews,'' he said, mentioning the name of the managing editor.

She knew she could count on him. Too bad there were no men out there like her father. ''Nice to have connections in low places,'' Sherry quipped.

Sin-Jin had always believed that the way to kill a rumor was to ignore it and allow it to die for lack of fuel.

The headline on the *Bulletin* he'd brought to Sherry's attention had irritated him, but he'd managed to shrug it off. He fully expected it to die like everything else. He was not about to demand a retraction or an apology. There was no way he was about to dignify the false story with any sort of reaction on his part.

So when Mrs. Farley came into his office two days later with another copy of the *Bulletin* in her hand, he made no offer to take it from her, even when she waved it at him.

He knew she always had his best interests at heart,

but there were times when she took the matter of his honor a little too personally.

"I'm really not interested in a follow-up, Mrs. Farley." Turning from his computer, he looked up at her. "I don't know why you bother with something like that."

Edna drew herself up to her full small stature. "I don't bother with it." Her tone was not defensive, just firm. "Joseph Bailey in accounting brought it to my attention. I really think you should look at page two."

He paused tolerantly. "Now why would I want to do that?"

She placed the paper on his desk, turning it to face him. "So that you can see history in the making. To my knowledge, this has never happened before in the *Bulletin.*"

Amusement raised one corner of his mouth. He glanced at the headline. "They have exclusive photographs of aliens taking over Alaska?"

"Better."

When he made no effort to open the paper, Mrs. Farley came around the desk. She opened the tabloid for him. Handling the paper gingerly, as if merely touching it defiled her fingertips, she turned to the second page. Moving it before him again, she jabbed her index finger at the box on the bottom of the page. "Read."

"Yes, ma'am," he joked. The tone of her voice placed them back in time some twenty years or so. He was in her English class again, getting help after hours. She'd been an unrelenting woman then, as she was now.

Placating her, he looked down to where she was pointing.

Amazed, he read the four lines again. And then he raised his eyes up to hers. Mrs. Farley was smiling. She rarely did that. "It's a retraction," he said.

"Yes, it is," she agreed triumphantly, taking the paper away again and folding it back into its original position. Victory had momentarily taken away the paper's taint.

Leaning back in his chair, he scrutinized the older woman. He'd obviously underestimated her. "How did you get them to do this?"

"I didn't. I just assumed that you did."

Sin-Jin laughed shortly. "You know better than to think I'd dignify a rag like the *Bulletin* with a phone call."

Pencil-thin light-brown eyebrows drew together in confusion as Mrs. Farley mulled over the situation. "Well, if you didn't, then who did?" She frowned as she dropped the tabloid into the wastepaper basket. "I doubt very much if anyone at that establishment has suddenly gotten a conscience. The people of the fourth estate are born without them."

The fourth estate.

Campbell.

Sin-Jin thought of the look on Sherry's face when he'd handed the single sheet to her. She'd looked surprised and then angry.

And, suddenly, he thought he had his answer.

Chapter Nine

Sherry heard the phone ringing from within her house as she put the key into the lock. Hurrying inside, she picked the receiver up on the third ring.

"Hello?"

"Did you do this?"

"Sin-Jin?" She tossed her purse on the sofa and kicked off her shoes before she sank down on the cushion. Her visit to her gynecologist had been uneventful. According to the woman, she was doing fine and all systems were go. She'd stopped at the hospital next to see her baby, wishing the same could be true of him. "You know, it's customary to say hello when you call someone."

"Hello." She heard something rustling on the other end of the line. "Did you do this?"

"And 'this' would be...?" She waited for him to

fill in the space. ''Don't forget, I'm good, but I'm not clairvoyant.''

There was a hint of impatience in his voice. The man had to be hell to work for, she decided. ''The retraction in the *Bulletin.* Are you the one behind it?''

Sherry curled her legs under her. She certainly hadn't expected this kind of reaction. ''You make it sound like an assassination plot. If you mean did I have something to do with having the *Bulletin* set the record straight, yes I did.''

Unable to bring herself to actually buy the tabloid, she'd asked Rusty to get a copy for her. He'd dropped it by the day after Sin-Jin had given her the front page. The article, full of speculations that were guardedly phrased, had been accompanied by a couple of rather unflattering shots of the two of them, very obviously spliced together from separate sources.

''Why did you bother?''

She frowned. ''A simple 'thank you' would have sounded better, but if you must know, I did it because I'm a journalist. I deal in the truth, not lies just because they guarantee sales.'' There was silence on the other end. ''Hello? You still there?''

After a beat, he answered. ''I'm still here. I'm just sitting here, trying to imagine your nose growing.''

She didn't know whether to be insulted or to laugh. ''I think you've made a mistake. Pinocchio's nose only grew when he lied. My nose is the same size it's always been, thank you.''

And it was a lovely nose, Sin-Jin caught himself thinking. Set in an even lovelier face.

He blew out a breath, impatient with himself. What the hell was going on with him? He didn't have time for this kind of mental drifting.

She shifted the receiver to her other ear. "Have you blown down the three little pigs' houses yet, or is there some other reason that you're huffing like the big, bad wolf?"

He frowned, still looking at the retraction. It placed him in a vulnerable position. Far more vulnerable than the original, silly article had. "If you think getting this retraction somehow places me in your debt—"

So that was it, he thought she wanted something from him. It figured. "Debt had nothing to do with it. Besides, if we're talking debt, I do owe you a favor." *Or six or seven,* she added silently. There was no way to repay what he had done for her son. It went far beyond his covering the hospital bills. Those she could well handle herself. Losing the baby was another matter.

He wanted to make his position perfectly clear. "I'm not in the business of exchanging favors."

It was always about him, wasn't it? This wasn't going anywhere. "Oh, no? My mistake." She wanted to hang up. "Look, if there's nothing else—"

He'd offended her, he thought, surprised at the regret that followed in the wake of the realization. Sin-Jin didn't want to leave it that way. After all, she had done him a service. "Sorry. I guess I'm just not into interpersonal exchanges."

Sherry softened slightly. She sensed that apologies didn't come easily to him. "They're called relationships, Sin-Jin, and don't worry, you're not in one. Our paths just crossed, that's all.''

''Right.'' Sin-Jin paused again, then added, ''Thank you.''

She felt warmth seeping in. Damn him, but he could turn her around faster than a weathervane swinging back and forth in a gale. ''You're welcome.''

She continued smiling long after she hung up the telephone.

He was home; her baby was home.

Finally.

Sherry had no idea she could feel this wide expanse of emotions running through her all at once. Relief, joy, pride, love, they were all bouncing around within her, temporarily blocking out the exhaustion that stood waiting in the wings.

Ever since she and her parents had brought her son home from the hospital six hours ago, the house had been laid siege to. There had been an endless stream of visitors from the moment they had arrived, all bearing gifts, all eager for a peek, however brief, of the tiny guest of honor.

John Connor Campbell lay in the white Jenny Lind crib bought for him by the ladies of The Mom Squad and assembled for him by his loving grandparents. All five and a half pounds of him.

Sherry lost count of how many times she came by just to look in on him.

He looked like an angel, dropping by for a visit. Sherry hoped that she would never think of him any other way. She doubted that she could. He was her special miracle.

Making her way back to the living room, she watched as her mother ushered the last visitor out. Sherry sank down on the sofa. The low buzz of noise that had surrounded her for the past six hours had finally faded. Her eyes drifting shut, she demurred when her mother said she was staying the night. She should have known better.

"I'm not taking no for an answer, Sherry Lynn Campbell." Opening her eyes, Sherry saw that her mother had fisted her hands at her sides, a sure sign that she was digging in. "We can send your father home, but I'll be staying here for the night." Sherry tried to protest, but only got as far as opening her mouth. Her mother headed her off at the pass. "There's no way I'm going to leave you all alone with a brand-new baby. You'll both be crying within the hour." As the woman moved about the room, straightening, she picked up the throw that had been set aside and spread it out over her daughter's legs. "If it hadn't been for my own mother, flying in from Ireland to be by my side those first few weeks I had you, I would have fallen to pieces. The least I can do is return the favor in her memory."

Sherry knew it was useless, but she felt bound to try. "Mom—"

Sheila fixed her daughter with a reproving look. "You wouldn't be wanting me to dishonor the memory of your sainted grandmother, now would you?"

Game, set and match, she thought. "No," Sherry sighed. "I wouldn't. If you're sure—"

Her mother didn't wait for the sentence to be completed. ''I'm sure.'' She looked at her husband. ''You can make your own dinner for a change, Connor. See what I have to put up with every night.''

Connor snorted. ''For your information, I'll be taking my supper at McIntyre's tonight.''

''Restaurant food. You know perfectly well they don't serve authentic Irish food at McIntyre's.'' Sheila sniffed disdainfully.

''Yes, my love,'' Connor replied patiently, ''and if I didn't, I'd have you to remind me of it.'' He gave his wife his most calculated pathetic look, the one only family got to see. ''But what's a poor man who can't boil water to do?''

Sherry couldn't keep it in any longer. She laughed. ''Mom, let him stay for supper.''

''But I thought you didn't want too many people around,'' her mother said.

''I didn't want to put you out,'' she corrected. ''And Dad's not people, he's Dad. Since you're here and I know you're going to cook for me no matter what I say, you might as well throw another plate on the table and have Dad stay, too.''

She'd never known her mother not to cook for ten and expect that people would just show up to avail themselves of leftovers. When Sherry was growing up, she'd been certain that she had a huge family. It surprised her to realize that there were only the three of them at the core and that all the others were just friends she'd grown up calling uncle and aunt. Friends who enjoyed the warm atmosphere created by Connor and Sheila Campbell.

''Well, if you insist, love,'' her father said magnanimously as he settled himself in on the other end of the sofa.

"I insist." The doorbell rang and her smile faded. She stared at it in disbelief. She'd had more visitors than comprised the populations of some small third-world countries. "I didn't know there was anyone left in Bedford who hadn't dropped by today."

"I'll get it," Sheila volunteered cheerfully. "You just rest yourself."

The instant his wife was out of the room, Connor leaned forward toward his daughter. "If she starts to drive you crazy tonight, just give me a call. I'll come for her in an instant."

It was shorthand for her father saying that he wasn't looking forward to spending the night without her mother by his side. She wondered how he'd managed all those years when he'd been sent to various places in the world on assignment. And more than that, she wondered if there would ever be that kind of relationship, that kind of love, waiting for her someday.

"The guest room's got a double bed, Dad." It was a needless piece of information. He'd seen her guest room. "Why don't you just stay the night here with Mom?"

Her father pretended to debate the matter. As an actor he would have starved, she thought in amusement. "I don't think she wants me interfering."

Her parents thrived on interfering with each other. "You can take turns changing the baby."

"Well, if you insist." He heard his wife's heels on the tile as she returned to the room. "Hey, Sheilo," he called her by the nickname he'd given her, "Sherry here says that I can stay and help if I behave. We'll take turns on the poop brigade."

"Dad!"

His daughter was looking over his head. Twisting around, he saw why Sherry looked so embarrassed. His wife was not alone.

Connor rose to his feet, extending his hand in a warm greeting. "Well, nice to see you again, Sin-Jin." He didn't bother hiding his smug expression. "Although I can't say I'm surprised."

Sherry wanted to sink into the sofa and just disappear. "Dad—"

"Well, I'm not," Connor protested. "A fella's not supposed to lie, is he?"

Sherry's father might not have been surprised to see him show up here, Sin-Jin thought, but he had to admit that he was. He hadn't expected to be anywhere near Sherry's home. But he'd gotten a call from the hospital's insurance administrator, per his earlier request, notifying him that the Campbell baby had been discharged that morning. Sin-Jin had had Mrs. Farley cut a voucher from his private funds for the proper amount of the account the moment he'd hung up. It was already in the mail.

The thought that "that was that" was somehow short-lived. It had faded in the wake of his desire to see how the child was faring.

If the mother happened to be in the same vicinity, well, so be it.

It was a flimsy excuse.

Sin-Jin realized that Connor was waiting for him to say something that would back him up. Obligingly, he allowed, "No, he's not. I can't say that I expected to be here, though.'' Feeling uncustomarily awkward, he looked down at the gaily wrapped box he was holding. Again, he had to thank Mrs. Farley, who knew exactly what to get. ''I brought the baby a little welcome home gift.''

Sherry took the box from him and removed the ribbon. And then laughed. It was a Green Bay Packers jersey, made for an infant. Even so, it looked almost too large for the baby. Something to grow into, she mused.

Tossing the box onto the sofa, she held the jersey up for her parents to see. ''Green Bay?''

Sin-Jin wasn't much into sports anymore, but he did follow the team's progress when he had the chance.

''It's a feisty team. I admire their spirit.'' He saw the look in Sherry's eyes and knew exactly what she was thinking. That he'd opened himself up a little more. The comment hardly deserved to be guarded. A lot of people liked the Green Bay Packers.

''I was just beginning to make dinner, Sin-Jin,'' Sheila informed him. ''You'll stay, of course.'' Sweetly extended, the invitation still left no room for refusal.

Sherry slanted a look toward him. She didn't want the man to feel trapped. Or worse, critical of these people she loved so dearly. ''Mom, I'm sure Sin-Jin has somewhere else to be.''

Sin-Jin thought about his own house, empty except for the housekeeper who always discreetly faded into the shadows, of the dinner he was going to partake in solitude. There was something about the way the three people in the room interacted, the body language he observed that created an atmosphere of warmth that pulled him in. It was like nothing he had experienced, certainly not within his own family.

The decision was spur-of-the-moment. "Oddly enough, I don't. Mrs. Farley thought I needed some free time."

"And Mrs. Farley is?" Connor asked.

"His secretary," Sherry quickly cut in just in case Sin-Jin was about to tell her father that it was none of his business. "She guards you with her life, you know. The first time I tried to get in to see you, she absolutely refused to allow it. Told me to call back at a more convenient time."

Sin-Jin smiled. "She tends to be a little protective. We go way back."

Tilting her head beguilingly, Sheila asked, "How far is that?"

"Far," Sin-Jin replied, amused. Apparently relentless questioning was a family trait.

Sherry grinned. "I think he's getting immune to you, Mom."

"The evening is still young," her mother replied with a wink directed at Sin-Jin. A tiny mewling sound came over the baby monitor that was placed in the center of the coffee table. Sheila exchanged glances with her husband. "I'm off for the kitchen, Connor. Think you can handle John?"

Sherry saw Sin-Jin's head jerk up at the mention of her son's name. He looked startled. Why?

"Piece of cake," Connor said confidently. Inclining his head toward Sin-Jin, he shared a confidence with pride. "See, I'm a modern man. Diapering, feeding, all those things."

"It's called teaching an old dog new tricks," Sheila said over her shoulder as she left the room, she going in one direction, her husband in another.

Alone, Sherry turned to look at Sin-Jin. He still appeared slightly bewildered. "You looked surprised."

"I, um—" Sin-Jin glanced toward the stairs.

And then she thought she understood. "I named him after you."

"Then his name is actually St. John?"

"No," she admitted. "Just John. I couldn't get myself to call him St. John, so I settled on John." Looking at him, she tried to envision what Sin-Jin had been like years ago. Probably still as formal. He probably wore crisply creased pants and blazers when he went to play. The image made her smile. "You must have endured a lot of teasing as a boy."

He looked at her blankly. His childhood had been marked with loneliness, not teasing. "Why?"

"Well, you can't say that 'St. John' is exactly an everyday name, now, can you? And kids always have a field day with people who are different."

He shrugged carelessly, thinking that perhaps he'd made a mistake, agreeing to remain. He should get going before the questions began in earnest. "I survived."

"Obviously." He looked like someone about to take flight, she thought. Probably regretting being roped into dinner. She needed to get this out before Sin-Jin suddenly made his apologies and left. "Anyway, now that you're here, I was wondering if I could ask you about something—"

All right, here it came. The payoff. He might have

known there was a reason behind the invitation and display of filial closeness. She'd been setting him up for the kill. "Look, don't get the wrong idea. I'm still not going to give you an interview—"

The cool rebuff had her pulling up short. "I'm not asking for an interview."

"Oh?" He didn't know whether to believe her and feel like a jackass, or applaud the way she could shift gears in midtransit.

She wasn't about to get caught in a lie. "At least, not right now." Owen had been very clear that he wanted her to take it easy. Any stories she was on could wait. It wasn't as if any of the stories were a matter of national security. "I'm on maternity leave and I intend to make the most of it."

He eyed her, waiting to see what she would come up with. "Then what's your question?"

"Will you be my son's godfather?"

"What?" The woman took the prize when it came to catching him off his guard.

"Godfather," she repeated, enunciating the word. "You know, someone who stands up for the baby at the baptism. Technically it's supposed to be someone of the same faith as you, but Father Conway is a good guy." She had known the white-haired priest for as long as she could remember. Going to church meant seeing the small, sprightly man, who looked very much like an elderly, transplanted elf, officiating at Mass. "He'll look the other way if Dad asks him to. What really counts here is the character of the godparent."

How could she even say that with a straight face? "You don't know anything about my character." He thought of all the scathing articles he'd read about himself. ''And what you do know doesn't exactly qualify me as an example for a young boy.''

She wasn't about to get swayed by the reports, especially now that she had had a chance to be around him. ''I know you wouldn't turn your back on a pregnant woman giving birth. That's enough for me. So will you?'' When Sin-Jin didn't respond immediately, she gave her own interpretation to his hesitation. ''I intend to live forever, so you don't have to worry about having to take care of Johnny, and even if I don't, my parents are ready to take him, so all that remains for you, really, is the honor of the thing.''

This had to be a gimmick of some kind. ''Why are you giving this 'honor' to me?''

She would have thought that was self-evident. She didn't like the suspicion in his eyes. ''Because if it wasn't for you,'' she said softly, ''my son wouldn't be here now.''

Without him noticing, she'd placed her hand on his arm in quiet supplication. He felt himself cornered. And not resenting it. ''You're not leaving me any space to turn you down.''

She smiled, the effect hitting him right between the eyes. ''That's the general idea.''

''All right, what do I have to do?''

She thought for a second. ''Be there at the church. Oh, and hold him while the priest sprinkles holy water on his forehead.''

There had to be more. ''What else?''

Sherry shook her head. ''That's all.''

He had no experience in these matters, but it definitely sounded too simple, too innocent. ‘‘I don’t even have to buy anything?’’

‘‘Nope.’’ She thought of her cousin who she’d asked the moment she knew she was carrying a child. Even before she told Drew. ‘‘The godmother takes care of the baby’s christening outfit.’’ She smiled up at him. ‘‘All you have to do is be there.’’

He wanted to leave himself a way out. ‘‘My schedule’s pretty booked.’’

She’d already found out that he worked a full week and sometimes added on a Saturday, but he kept Sundays to himself. ‘‘It’ll be on a Sunday afternoon.’’

She was good, he’d have to give her that. ‘‘Got all the answers ready, don’t you?’’

‘‘I always try.’’ She tried to read his expression. ‘‘So, what do you say?’’

He couldn’t have explained why this felt as if it was a huge commitment on his part, but it was, even though she had just told him it wasn’t. He wanted to choose his commitments, not have them presented to him.

‘‘I’m not—’’

Sherry shrugged. She wasn’t about to beat him over the head and drag him to the church.

‘‘Well, the honor belongs to you. If you can’t make it, my dad’ll be there in your place, like a stand-in. But your name’s going on the certificate. Don’t worry, there’re no strings,’’ she assured him again. ‘‘We don’t want anything from you. It’s just my way of saying thank you.’’

Had she argued, he might have stood a chance. Her dignified retreat had left him with an odd feeling of guilt that he was far from familiar with. Under the circumstances, he said the only thing he could.

"I'll be there."

Hiding her triumph, Sherry only smiled and said, "That's great."

Sin-Jin couldn't have cited why, but he felt like the man who had just signed on the dotted line and handed over a deposit on the Brooklyn Bridge.

Chapter Ten

Sin-Jin couldn't remember the last time that the minutes had just slipped away, knitting themselves into hours without his having monitored their departure by periodically glancing at his watch. He hadn't looked at the worn timepiece once. The company around him was too compelling.

Accustomed to conversations that dealt with fair market values of products, the international worth of the dollar and the recent history of various stocks, listening to personal stories about the woman sitting beside him and the trials of a marriage that seemed to have been made in heaven instead of hell—the marketplace of both his parents' numerous unions—was an unusual change, to say the least.

Sin-Jin found himself being reeled in until he felt as if he'd known Sheila and Connor Campbell for years rather than for hardly any time at all. And through them, Sherry.

His uncle would have liked these people.

The realization had quietly sneaked up on him from the deep recesses of his mind. He hadn't thought very much about Uncle Wayne lately. Probably because he didn't want to dwell on what his uncle might have had to say about the direction his life had taken over these past ten years or so. The world he had come to inhabit was more like the one his father existed in than the one his uncle had been dedicated to.

The thought bothered him more than he liked to admit.

"Another helping of dessert, Sin-Jin?" On her feet, Sheila was already cutting another slice of chocolate cream pie, confident of the response.

The dinners he was used to partaking of were artfully arranged meals surrounded by a great deal of plate. He'd astonished himself tonight by the amount of food he'd consumed. There'd been two helpings of the main course, followed by the same amount of servings of dessert. He was already in danger of needing the jaws of life to remove him from his clothing.

"No, really, I've eaten a great deal more than I usually do."

Connor eyed their guest, then chuckled. "You're one of those people who eats to live, aren't you?" He snaked his arm around his wife's middle, drawing her closer to him as he sat at the table. Sheila squealed, swatted his arm away. But she remained standing beside him, her expression that of a woman who was loved and pleased to allow the world to know it. "I was like that myself until Sheila here came into my life."

Sheila winked broadly at her guest. "Married me for my cooking."

"Hell, woman," Connor snorted, "if I'd just wanted you for what you could do in the kitchen, I would have hired you instead of giving you my name."

Sheila sniffed, tossing her head, the ends of her hair brushing along her slim shoulders. "You didn't give it, I deigned to take it."

Connor sighed, shaking his head as he looked at Sin-Jin. "Modern women, it's a wonder any of us men have managed to survive 'em."

"Sure I can't tempt you?" Having cut a healthy slice of the pie, Sheila now held it just above his plate, ready to set it down.

It was time for Sherry to come to the rescue before the man beside her became annoyed, overwhelmed or exploded. "No means no, Mom. Stop feeding him before we have to roll him out the door." Sherry turned to Sin-Jin. "Mom's destiny, she thinks, is to fatten up the immediate world."

Temporarily surrendering, Sheila placed the slice on her husband's dessert plate instead. She gave Sherry the once-over. "You could stand to gain a pound or seven, yourself, missy. Seems now that the baby's out, you're your former too-thin self."

"I think she looks just fine."

Three sets of eyes turned to look at him. Sin-Jin coughed, realizing that once again he'd said too much. It was getting to be an unnerving habit around anyone named Campbell.

"Would you mind if I took a peek at my godson-to-be?"

My God, one evening in their company and he was even beginning to sound like these people. He didn't dwell on how odd it felt to refer to any child as his godson. He'd long ago stopped thinking of the concept of any sort of family, even an extended one. Since he had no example to look back on, he couldn't trust himself to be involved in any relationship that wasn't doomed to fail right from the start. And he wasn't about to bring a child into the world to have only half a family. Besides, what did he know about children anyway?

She knew a call for help when she heard one. "I thought you'd never ask." The baby had required one feeding since Sin-Jin had arrived. She'd excused herself while her father had held Sin-Jin captive with one of his long-winded stories. When she'd returned, she'd been surprised to find that Sin-Jin hadn't bolted. Sherry rose to her feet, pushing back her chair. "Right this way."

Following behind Sherry, Sin-Jin missed the knowing look that was exchanged by her parents, but as she turned on the stairs, Sherry had caught it. She knew that for once her parents, in their unfailing optimism, were dead wrong.

She opened the door to the baby's room and motioned Sin-Jin inside. It amused her that he seemed to be tiptoeing in. Leaning his arms on the railing, he looked down at the sleeping baby.

"He looks tinier than when I saw him in the hospital," he whispered to her.

The whisper, low and sexy, seemed to slip along her skin. She leaned her head toward him just a little to keep from having to raise her voice to be heard.

"That's because the crib dwarfs him." He did look tiny, she thought. She'd already nicknamed him "peanut," but that was going to have to change by the time he was old enough to understand. She wasn't about to give her child any deep-rooted psychological problems because of a pet name. "It just means he'll get more use out of his clothes."

Sin-Jin was amazed. There were people who would be beside themselves in the same situation she was in, already booking specialists for their infant. Yet Sherry seemed calm and confident. "You always think so positively?"

There was a smile in her eyes when she looked at him. "Always. Focusing on the negative never makes you anything but unhappy. It certainly never gets you anywhere."

"It prepares you for things when they go wrong."

She turned toward him. "But if they don't go wrong, think of all the time you've wasted, despairing."

"And if they do go wrong?" he challenged.

"Well," she said, shrugging philosophically, "then at least you've had a little hope in your life to make you feel better."

The woman certainly wasn't an idiot, and yet, as intelligent as she was, she still managed to be optimistic. Coming from a world grounded in reality and worst-case scenarios, he found her attitude unsophisticated—and incredibly appealing.

Maybe it was time to leave.

Sherry saw him looking at his watch and was struck not just by the fact that a great deal of time had gone by and he was still here, but by the watch itself, as well. She would have expected someone with Sin-Jin's affluent lifestyle and penchant for the finest that life had to offer to be wearing a Rolex, or at least a similar ludicrously expensive watch. Instead he was wearing a watch whose face had seen better days and whose metallic black band was worn and tarnished in several places. It seemed entirely against type.

Sin-Jin saw her looking at his wristwatch. He lowered the cuff of his jacket back into place, not to hide the watch but to protect it.

"It was my uncle's."

That was the second time he'd actually mentioned a family member to her. "The same uncle who was a doctor?"

She'd been in the throes of pain when he'd said that to her. He was amazed that she remembered. "You don't miss a thing, do you?"

Taking his arm, she led him out of the room and back to the stairs. "I try not to. Am I right?"

She fell into place far too easily beside him. Alarms should have been going off, but they remained dormant. Why was that, he wondered. "Yes, he left it to me when he died."

"Doesn't seem like much of a legacy."

He thought of the one photograph of his uncle he carried in his wallet. The man had looked like an aging hippie, long gray hair pulled back in a ponytail, a beard and worn work shirt and jeans that had more than seen their day of service. The man had meant more to him than all his other relatives combined. "His legacy wasn't in material things."

"And he was a doctor?"

Sin-Jin walked down the stairs in front of her. "The kind that goes off to practice medicine in the poorest sections of the country because that's where he's needed the most."

He didn't add that when his uncle was preparing to leave for the Appalachian area, Sin-Jin had been all of ten years old. He'd begged the man not to go, saying that he needed him to stay in his life. His uncle had talked to him for hours, finally making him realize that there were children who needed him even more than he did. It was the first time he'd been confronted with the concept of charitable giving.

Sin-Jin turned to look at Sherry, who had stopped at the base of the stairs. Her expression was thoughtful. He did what he could in the way of damage control, berating himself for having mentioned anything. "He was kind of the black sheep of the family."

Not so black, Sherry thought. And he'd meant something to Sin-Jin. Anyone with ears would know that. "What happened to him?"

Sin-Jin's face sobered. "He died."

There was a note of finality in his voice that forbade her asking any more questions.

She was curious even beyond her realm of investigative reporter, wanting to know particulars of the man's life before his death, but she wasn't insensitive. For now she let the matter drop.

"So you said. Well," she said, glancing toward the living room. They were going to have to run the gauntlet in order to get to the front door. "Let me walk you to the door and help make good your escape before my father suddenly thinks to engage you in a 'friendly game of poker.'" She saw Sin-Jin raise an eyebrow in silent query. "Believe me, it's not all that friendly. My father hates to lose. At anything. It's his one flaw."

"A lot of men are like that."

Was he putting her on some kind of notice? "Including you?"

His eyes held hers. "Including me."

She felt a shiver of electricity dance along her skin, but held her ground.

"Then you had really better not get in a card game with him." She saw her parents already turning in their direction. "Ready?" she murmured.

She made him feel as if he was about to navigate the rapids in a paper raft and no paddle. Rather than answer, he made his way into the living room.

Sheila was the first to meet him halfway. "Oh, but you're not really leaving."

"Mom, if he stays here any longer, his people'll probably be expecting a ransom note of some kind to be delivered."

"Well..." Moving forward, Sheila enveloped him in a warm embrace that caught him completely by surprise. "If you must, you must." Stepping back, she looked genuinely disappointed that he wasn't staying longer.

Ordinarily when people tried to detain him, it was to talk about business, to try to get him to back a deal, or something equally based on money. The look on Sheila Campbell's face was rooted in emotion. It stirred feelings that he had long ago placed under lock and key, when he'd decided that he was not destined to have the kind of family he ached for.

The kind of family Sherry had.

Connor wasn't as easily put off. He placed his arm around Sin-Jin's shoulders, having to reach up a little as he did so. ''Sure I can't talk you into a friendly little card game?''

Sherry quickly wedged herself in between the two men, brushing against Sin-Jin in order to do it. She seemed to be oblivious to the contact. No such lapse was experienced on his side. The lady's soft contours telegraphed themselves to him with the speed of lightning traveling up a rod.

''It won't work, Dad,'' she informed her father. ''I've already warned Sin-Jin about your friendly little games.''

Connor frowned. ''Whatever she said, she was exaggerating.'' He nodded his head toward his wife. ''Gets that from her mother, she does.''

Sheila pretended to be incensed, crossing her arms over her chest, her accent thick enough to rival the pie she'd served earlier. ''I'll be begging your pardon, sir, but you're the one given to blarney, not me.''

Connor turned, laughing as he caught his wife up in his arms and kissed her soundly. ''And you love it.''

Sheila rested her head against her husband's shoulder. The two formed a contented picture. ''Never said I didn't, did I?''

Taking Sin-Jin's arm, Sherry ushered him to the door. ''I think you'd better go before your stomach decides to rebel against what you've just witnessed. They only get worse with encouragement.''

''Sherry Lynn Campbell,'' her mother protested, ''what a thing to say. And before a guest, too.''

''True,'' Sherry testified, ''every word of it.''

Escorting him to the door, she surprised him by closing it behind them. She walked with him to his car in the driveway.

''Your parents seem very nice.''

She smiled. There were times they embarrassed her, but she loved them both dearly. If they hadn't been there for her in the beginning months, she didn't know what she would have done.

''There's no 'seem' about it.'' She looked toward the house. ''They *are* nice. I couldn't have asked for a better set—'' Her mouth curved in self-deprecation as she remembered. ''Something I wasn't all that sure of twelve years ago.''

He took a guess. It wasn't that much of a stretch. ''The rebellious years?''

She inclined her head in semiassent. ''Something like that. I'm surprised they didn't raffle me off to the highest bidder.''

He caught himself thinking he would have liked to have been part of that auction.

Suddenly feeling oddly self-conscious beneath his scrutiny, she ran her hands along her arms. ''Well...thanks for coming by, and I'm sorry if they came on a little strong. That's just their way.''

There was no need to apologize for her parents. He only wished that there had been a mold and that his could have been formed from the same one. ''Actually, I found it kind of refreshing.''

''Even though my dad's a former reporter?''

''Even though,'' Sin-Jin acknowledged. The man didn't seem like any reporter he'd ever met. But then, he was beginning to think the same thing about Sherry. All the reporters who had crossed his path were like sharks, waiting for the first sign of blood. ''Besides, the key word here is *former.* Can't hold things against someone forever.''

She didn't want to go inside just yet. Didn't want to see him leave. ''So you hold my vocation against me?''

What he wanted to hold against her, he realized, was himself.

But he gave her the answer he knew she was expecting. The answer he would have been expecting himself—except now he wasn't completely certain of it any longer. ''As long as you keep your pen sheathed, we're all right.''

As a rule, Sin-Jin wasn't a man given to impulses, not since he'd walked away from his life all those many years ago and forged a new one for himself. Not until Sherry had burst into his life with the force of an unexpected squall at sea.

Impulse was guiding him now.

Again.

Maybe it was the moonlight caressing her skin. Maybe it was the warm environment he'd just left, an environment that had, however temporarily, broken down his barriers.

Or maybe it was the woman herself, half annoying, half enticing and completely exciting.

Whatever the explanation behind his actions, Sin-Jin found himself wanting to kiss her again.

And then he found himself kissing her.

The wanting didn't go away.

Sherry thought that this time she was ready. Braced. Forewarned was forearmed and all that.

It turned out to be the kind of slogan that did better inside a fortune cookie than out in the real world, because she wasn't forearmed, not in the slightest. What she was, instantly, was intoxicated.

One taste of the man's mouth had her wanting more, even though denial had been her constant companion since the last time he'd kissed her. She'd told herself then that it had just been a fluke. That having lived a life that would have bored a nun was responsible for her intense reaction to the man.

She'd told herself lies.

The moan that escaped her lips was involuntary.

Hearing it created an even greater rush in Sin-Jin's system than the taste of her lips already had. His body heating, he slipped his hands from her face to her shoulders, holding her closer to him. And then his arms went around her. Drawing her essence inside.

This had to stop.

He wasn't sure why.

Like a swimmer submerged for too long, his lungs aching, his body tingling, Sin-Jin came up for air. Taking a breath, he looked down at her. Funny, she didn't look like a witch. And then he thought of the Sirens. The mermaids who called sailors to their doom. *The Odyssey,* wasn't it? One of the books Mrs. Farley had assigned him to read so many years ago. They'd been beautiful, too. Beautiful but deadly, to be avoided at all costs.

So why wasn't he avoiding Sherry?

He had a hunch he knew why. "I have two tickets to the opening of a new performing-arts theater my company recently acquired and renovated. They're for two weeks from Saturday." Though the gala affair called for his attendance, he'd already made up his mind to give the tickets away. Until just now. "It's not a command performance or anything—"

"I'd love to." Afraid that he would change his mind before he finished asking the question, she fired her answer faster than a bullet.

He almost laughed. If he didn't know any better, he would have said she was eager. "We can have dinner first."

Sherry nodded. She knew her parents would be more than willing to baby-sit. They'd both been after her to resume her usual routine. "Sounds good to me."

"All right, then."

Getting into his car, he drove away. The official story he gave himself was that he was trying to cure himself of her. The best way was to sleep with her. Once the thrill of the conquest was over, he would be ready to move on. It always worked that way for him when it came to business. He saw no reason why it wouldn't work with this woman. It was a matter of self-preservation. He needed a clear head to conduct his work, and she was definitely blurring things for him. Ever since that day up at the cabin, he felt like a crayon that was continually being forced to draw outside the lines.

Sherry's heart was still pounding hard as she slipped back inside the house. Her parents were off in the kitchen and for that she was extremely grateful. She needed the time to pull herself together.

It took her a moment to get her bearings. Taking a deep breath and then releasing it slowly, the way she'd been taught to in Lamaze class, she took out the small pad she kept in her pocket. The pad she'd been carrying around ever since Owen had first given her this assignment. Drawing in another deep breath to steady her pulse, she jotted down the latest information Sin-Jin had inadvertently given her. She might be on maternity leave, but that didn't shut down the journalist in her.

"Uncle's name was Wayne. Doctor. Practiced in Appalachia."

Slowly but surely she was determined to piece together Sin-Jin's life—to form at least a shadow of the man he was. She slipped the pad back into her pocket. If she felt a little sneaky doing this, she consoled herself with the fact that he knew exactly what she was and no one was holding a gun to his head to tell her things.

Besides, she wasn't about to put this all down for Owen's perusal until she'd secured Sin-Jin's permission. When she was ready, and there was still a great deal of investigative work to be conducted, she was just going to have to find the right way to present the article to Sin-Jin.

But there was still time to worry about that.

Though two weeks away, she had to worry about

what on earth she was going to wear to a performing-arts theater opening.

She felt a bubble of excitement rising up within her. Cinderella was going to the ball. And Prince Charming was driving the coach.

Chapter Eleven

Cinderella had definitely come into her own, Sherry thought as she and Sin-Jin slowly made their way across the red carpet into the Bedford Performing Arts Theater Saturday evening.

The last time she'd seen so many women bedecked in diamonds, furs and designer gowns that came in the four-figure and up range, she'd been covering an Academy Awards function with Rusty for her television station. Then it had been an assignment, now she was supposedly on the inside, one of the beautiful people.

She wasn't vain enough to feel that she could carry off the pose comfortably.

For one thing her dress came with a far less impressive pedigree, an off-the-rack gown emerging from a local department store. Feeling a little self-conscious, she looked down at it.

"I think I'm a little underdressed," she whispered to Sin-Jin.

He escorted her through the door. The woman was garnering looks without even realizing it. Her strapless evening gown was high in the front, but dipped low as it made its way to her back, a perfect display of sexy modesty.

Inclining his head, he brought his lips to her ear. "From where I'm standing, you could do with a little more underdressing." She turned her head to look at him, her hair brushing against his face. He wasn't quite able to read the expression on her face. "Sorry, I couldn't resist. You look sensational."

The foyer, with its mirrors that doubled and tripled the number of people within its enclosure, added to the noise and confusion around her. His compliment surprised her. Pleasure embraced her. "I didn't think you noticed what I was wearing."

He slipped his arm around her waist, guiding her toward an open pocket of space. "Then obviously you think I'm far more cold-blooded than my rank detractors do." He allowed his eyes to travel slowly over the length of her, enjoying the journey. "An Egyptian mummy would have noticed what you were wearing, Sherry."

The shimmering hot-pink dress was only a breath away from being painted on, highlighting all of her curves and threatening to bring a lesser man to his knees. The floor-length gown's thigh-high slit didn't help his sense of concentration any.

He'd thought of her as attractive and distracting before. Now she was positively breathtaking.

And tonight, Sin-Jin promised himself, he was going to get her out of his system. After all, he was his father's son and as such given to noticing outstandingly attractive women. Sherry Campbell definitely fell into that category.

But the working rule of thumb was, once a conquest was met, it ceased to work its magic, ceased to hold its allure. He'd seen it time and again when he was growing up. His parents would become obsessed with someone, only to have that obsession fade once it became so-called permanent. He followed the same pattern, except that his passion was business. But there was no reason to believe it would be otherwise with a woman.

Still, he had to admit that he found the blush that crept up her neck vastly appealing, not to mention tantalizing. It made him want to trace the light pink path from its source.

Sherry scanned the area. Well-manicured, pampered bodies as far as the eye could see. ''Who are all these people?'' she wanted to know. ''Business acquaintances of yours?''

He knew a great many by name and by sight. And usually felt alone at these functions. That was why he was originally going to pass on this one.

''Some are, others refer to themselves as patrons of the arts. They're here to rub elbows with other patrons, to hear themselves hailed as 'angels,' and possibly last of all, to enjoy the show.''

She'd just thought that this was going to be some sort of dedication ceremony, filled with self-congratulations and adulation for Sin-Jin as the force behind the theater's stylish resurrection. ''So there is going to be a performance?''

Again he inclined his head. He was watching her expression too much, he admonished himself. After all, this could be used as a time to network further. ''A special, one-night, by-invitation-only, performance.''

She'd yet to see anyone handing out programs. ''Do I get a clue as to what it'll be, or am I going to be kept in the dark?''

He'd been informed ahead of time as to the program. He envisioned the letter he'd received several weeks ago. ''Highlights of the upcoming season, performed by every famous celebrity the director of the theater could round up.''

''And your company bought this theater and renovated it?'' The structure was all glass and glitter, the architectural, futuristic vision of an up-and-coming designer who was already making a name for himself. She'd discovered, by doing a little preliminary digging, that rather than work with what was, Sin-Jin'd had the old building torn down and reconstructed from the ground up. The end result was a thing of beauty that in some places seemed to defy gravity.

Business, the driving force in his life, felt somehow dull and boring to him tonight. ''We hold the mortgage.''

She smiled at the short, staccato sentence. ''Is that the collective 'we' or the royal 'we'?''

Instead of answering, Sin-Jin plucked a glass of champagne from the tray held out by a passing waiter and placed it in her hand. ''Here, see if this can get you to stop asking questions for a few minutes.''

She took a sip, her eyes on his. He felt that stirring

in his gut that he was beginning to associate with being around her. "Don't you like women with inquiring minds, Sin-Jin?"

Actually, he didn't. Until now. She was the rule breaker. It was becoming the norm with her. "Only if I can be sure that they're asking for themselves and not a potential reading audience."

"Touché." Sherry lifted her glass in a silent toast to him before taking another sip.

"Why, Sin-Jin, you did make it after all. Good for you."

The smooth British accent belonged to a distinguished-looking man who was dressed in a formal tuxedo, complete with arm candy. The woman he'd brought was young enough to be his daughter.

Which was, Sherry discovered several minutes later, exactly who the young woman was.

For the next forty-five minutes, until they were politely requested to go into the theater proper and take their seats, what seemed like an endless stream of people flowed by them, all wanting to spend a moment with someone they deemed to be one of the most influential men in the current business world. Sin-Jin conducted himself like someone to the manor born.

He was, she noted, charming to all of them. But even so, there remained that small distance between him and whoever he was talking to, that small distance that established him as ruler of his domain and testified that anyone he spoke with was just a separate island that was drifting by.

It was clearly his evening. And he had chosen to share it with her. Pretty heady stuff, Sherry mused.

Even headier was that he introduced her to people as exactly who she was, ar eporter for the *Bedford World News.* That in of itself garnered her more than one surprised look.

The moment the first bell chimed, alerting them to the fact that there were five minutes until the curtain went up, Sherry felt his hand slip to the small of her back.

"Time to go in," he told her. "And none too soon," he murmured under his breath.

She wasn't sure if he was addressing the remark to her, or if she just happened to overhear him talk to himself. Was he weary of these people who tried to curry his favor? When did the attention stop being flattery and become tedious?

One of the red-jacketed ushers showed them to their seats. They were located front-row center. Sherry was duly impressed.

"Wow, it certainly pays to hang around you." Taking her seat, she looked at Sin-Jin. God, but he did have a hell of a good-looking profile, she thought. "Does everyone always fall all over themselves around you?"

His eyes when he turned them on her made her feel as if she was the only one in the room. "You don't."

"I don't want anything—" She saw his eyebrow go up. Just one. Why was that so incredibly sexy? "All right," she relented, "except for an interview."

"You might want something," he observed, "but you're not pandering."

She lifted a slim, bare shoulder, then let it drop.

He found himself wanting to skim his fingers along the curve of skin. ''It's not my way.''

She was right. As annoyingly determined as she had come on, Sherry hadn't been about to flatter him in order to get what she wanted. Maybe that, he thought as the lights began to dim and he settled back, was why he was attracted to her.

In any case, it would be over with soon.

''You seemed to be living every beat of that music.'' The house lights were going up, signaling an intermission. He'd been watching her almost as much as he'd been watching the performers. He couldn't recall seeing anyone enjoy themselves as much as she was.

''I love musicals.'' She wasn't embarrassed to make the statement. She got her love of music from her father, who had sung with the church choir as a boy and had sung her to sleep with old beer-drinking songs he'd learned in his youth. ''There's something wondrous about feeling the beat vibrating in your chest. It makes you feel as if you were part of what was happening.''

The last number before intermission had been one lifted from *West Side Story.* ''Doesn't seeing a gang member suddenly break into song and execute intricate dance steps offend your sense of reality?''

She had a very healthy sense of reality—and enjoyed tucking it away on occasion. ''Nope. It enhances it.''

''Come again?''

Unless he felt the same way, she didn't think that he could begin to understand what she was talking about, but she gave it a try anyway. "Watching things like *West Side Story* and *Riverdance* make reality bearable to me sometimes."

He shook his head, amused. "If you say so."

What kind of person was this woman sitting beside him? Sin-Jin had to admit his curiosity about her surprised him. Under normal circumstances he would have sworn he didn't have a curious bone in his body.

And yet questions about her were occurring to him at an alarming rate. Questions such as why the father of her child wasn't at her side. She'd never mentioned the man to him, or commented about his absence.

It was ironic. For all her chatter, she seemed to be as private a person as he was.

The performance, complete with one intermission and three encores, lasted a little more than three hours. And then it took them almost another forty-five minutes to make their way out of the three-story building, even though he tried to hurry along their progress to the entrance.

Everyone, she noted, was determined to secure their five minutes with him. Twice he flashed an apologetic look in her direction. That he gave any thought at all to her comfort both intrigued and pleased her.

She amused herself by listening. When the jargon became too technical and boring, Sherry turned her attention to the handsomely bound program she'd been handed just before taking her seat the first time. What caught her attention were the last three pages.

They were completely devoted to the names of donors who had given generously to the foundation that was to oversee the immediate management of the theater.

Skimming over the list, it surprised her to see a familiar name. John Fletcher was one of the chief contributors, his name printed in the group of donors who were categorized as being in the Platinum Club, reflecting donations over a hundred thousand dollars. She wondered if it was the same John Fletcher whose cabin Sin-Jin had gone to. It was obvious that the man was as wealthy as Sin-Jin.

Was this John Fletcher a boyhood friend? A silent partner?

Sherry could feel her mind waking as possibilities began to suggest themselves to her. She began making mental notes.

"Tired?"

Lost in thought, the sound of his voice took a moment to penetrate. She realized that she'd just stifled a yawn. But that had nothing to do with him.

"No, I'm fine."

"You're yawning," he pointed out.

She was trying not to pay attention to the way his breath on her neck made her skin tingle. "New mothers don't get to sleep much."

Rather than say something along the lines that it would only be a few more minutes, he cut short his conversation with the latest group of men who had tried to commandeer his time.

"Sorry, I'm afraid that Ms. Campbell needs to make an early night of it."

"That's right," she said as he took her arm and

made for the exit again, "make me the bad guy." She glanced at her watch. It was just a little after midnight. "I guess I really am Cinderella," she murmured.

The air was bracing as they finally made it outside. Sin-Jin handed the valet his ticket before turning in her direction. When he did, there was amusement in his eyes. "You feel like Cinderella?"

She went for the obvious rather than tell him that she'd felt that way for most of the evening. "It's just a little after midnight."

How was it that she looked even better to him now than she had when he'd first picked her up at her home? "Does this mean that your dress is going to disappear?"

He was flirting with her, she thought. Something else she wouldn't have thought he was capable of. Sherry laughed. "Don't look so hopeful."

His look made her feel warm.

"I don't believe in missing opportunities."

The car arrived just then. She silently blessed the valet. The young man hurried out of the vehicle and went to hold the door open for her.

She slid in and waited until Sin-Jin got behind the wheel. "You were very patient tonight."

He turned the engine on, not sure what she was driving at. "With anyone in particular?"

That was just it. "With everyone."

Just what kind of image did she have of him? "Did you expect me to snarl?"

She looked at his profile for a long moment as he wove his Mercedes into the stream of traffic and they joined the slow-moving process of vehicles that were trying to make good their escape from the parking lot.

"I'm not exactly sure what I expect you to do anymore."

He kept his eyes forward. That makes two of us, he thought.

Rubbing the sleep from her eyes, Sheila looked surprised to see them walk into the house. She checked her watch to make sure she hadn't lost track of time and fallen asleep. Twelve-thirty. She felt disappointment unfurling inside her.

Getting off the sofa, she crossed to the foyer and met them halfway. "I wasn't expecting you back until two or three in the morning." She saw Sherry glance toward the stairs. It brought back memories of her own waltz with new motherhood and made her smile. "The baby's fine. I just put him down."

Sherry did a quick mental calculation. That gave her four hours before he woke up again—give or take an hour. She sincerely hoped her son was in a generous mood. Then again, she was probably not going to get any sleep tonight, not in her present wired state.

She smiled her gratitude at her mother. "I really appreciate this, Mom."

Her purse in hand, Sheila was already making for the front door. She was obviously anxious to leave the two of them alone. "Anytime."

Sherry slanted a glance toward Sin-Jin. Rather than leave her on her doorstep, he'd come inside with her when she'd unlocked the door. Nerves began to do pirouettes through her. If her mother left, she'd be alone with him. Alone with a man who'd flattered her, who'd flirted with her, and who she found immensely attractive.

Everything in her system cried out Mayday. Sherry looked to her mother for help, knowing it was probably as futile as grabbing on to a soda straw while drowning in the ocean. "Mom, you don't have to run out the second we walk in."

Her hand on the doorknob, Sheila was already opening the front door. "Now that he's retired, your father hates to sleep alone."

Sherry frowned. The excuse didn't jibe with her mother's earlier statement. "But you just said that you expected me to be in by three o'clock."

Rather than try to regroup, Sheila merely gave her daughter a patient, loving look. "It's too late to argue, sweetheart." Crossing back quickly, she kissed her daughter's cheek, whispered, "Have fun," in her ear and sailed back to the front door. She was gone in an instant.

Sherry stared after her mother as the door closed, a sinking feeling taking up residence in the pit of her stomach. The rest of her was humming with an anticipation she was trying vainly not to acknowledge.

"What did she say?"

She turned around, a little startled to discover that there was no space between them. She didn't remember Sin-Jin being this close a moment ago. Had the room gotten smaller somehow?

"She told me to have fun."

She pressed her lips together, telling herself she was being childish. It wasn't as if she was a vestal virgin and besides, he probably wasn't going to do anything anyway.

Nerves warred with disappointment.

"I guess she's more tired than she thinks," she told him.

His smile was slow, seeping into her system, covering every part of her like honey over ice cream. "Or more alert than you think."

Suddenly, the air around her became very still. She could hear every sound the house made. The slight creaking of the walls as the wind picked up. The sound of crickets outside the living room window, calling to one another, intent on having a mating fest.

Did crickets get lonely, too?

The single word shimmered before her. *Too.*

Her mouth had gone dry. Damn it, she *did* feel like a vestal virgin. What was the matter with her? "She always has been a sharp lady."

He threaded one hand through her hair, cupping her cheek. Making strange things happen to her insides. "You looked very beautiful tonight. Or did I already tell you that?"

It took her a moment to get in enough air to answer. "You did. Past tense?"

His smile widened, pure pleasure marking the path. He had a really nice smile, she thought, feeling herself losing ground. "Past, present, pluperfect, take your choice."

Breathe, damn it, breathe. "Are you going to kiss me again?"

He shook his head slightly, his eyes never leaving hers. "Don't you ever stop asking questions?"

"I...don't think...I know...how." The words

seemed to dribble from her lips, dew slowly sliding down the petals of a rose.

"Let me see if I can help you with that." He brought his mouth down to hers, sealing in her questions and releasing a wave of excitement that felt almost overwhelming.

The kiss was gentle, sweet. The more receptive she became to it, the more it grew until it felt as if there wasn't a single space left that wasn't filled by the kiss or by the emotions it generated within her.

Sherry leaned into him, their bodies touching then pressing against each other as their breaths mingled and their tongues tangled. Desire sprang up, full-bodied and strong, embracing her.

Her eyes shut, Sherry fell headlong into the kiss, losing her bearings. Not wanting to find them again. At least, not yet.

Her heart was pounding hard as she felt his warm hands slide along her shoulders, her back. Melting her knees. Making her quiver inside.

And then there was separation. He was drawing his head back, leaving her adrift. When she opened her eyes, she saw that there was just the slightest look of uncertainty in his. St. John Adair, uncertain? It didn't seem possible.

"Maybe I should go."

No! The wave of panic almost took her breath away as much as the kiss had. "It can't be anything I've said because I think I just swallowed my tongue."

He found her honesty incredibly refreshing. Sin-Jin was beginning to think that she was a rare woman. ''No, but maybe I'm rushing things.'' She had, after all, just given birth a few weeks ago.

Sherry placed her hands on his arms, looking up at him. It was as if she no longer had a choice in this, that her destiny was already preordained, written down in some vast book somewhere.

''Isn't that what makes you so good at what you do? You know when to rush in and when not?''

Normally, he thought. But right now, he'd seemed to have lost his instincts. They'd evaporated, leaving him feeling just the slightest bit lost. It wasn't something he was used to.

The thought that fools rush in where angels fear to tread meandered through his mind. ''I'm afraid that this time I need a little input. Did the doctor say—'' He never got a chance to finish his question.

According to her gynecologist after her exam, everything was back in working order and better than ever. ''The doctor says I'm terrific.'' Sherry pulled herself up on her toes and brought her lips up to his, kissing him for all she was worth.

''Yes,'' he murmured against her mouth, ''you certainly are.''

He could feel her lips widen into a smile. A smile that imprinted itself on his soul.

''I never thought I'd hear myself say this, Sin-Jin, but you talk too much.''

Sin-Jin laughed, sweeping her up into his arms. ''Let's see what we can do about that.''

And then the laughter faded.

Chapter Twelve

He was seducing her.

From the moment he first kissed her, the seduction began, enveloping her, making her tingle with incredible anticipation.

There were all sorts of things wrong with this. The words *conflict of interest* sprang up in her mind in eight-foot-high letters. This was a dalliance, a temporary meeting of bodies, for him. She knew that. It had no future, not even the hint of a promise of a future.

She had to be out of her mind.

She'd just come away from a three-year relationship that had self-destructed on her, and here she was, seeking shelter in the arms of a man who had a billfold where his heart was supposed to be.

Everything was wrong with this picture. And only one thing was right.

She wanted it to happen.

Maybe she needed to believe, just for the space of a few hours, that she was desirable, that she was wanted by someone. By a man who could easily, as she had seen tonight, have absolutely any woman he wanted with just a snap of his fingers.

So what was she doing, being the one he snapped for?

And yet…

And yet he hadn't snapped. He'd given her a way out. A way she didn't want to take.

If he was using her for pleasure tonight, well, she was using him as well, using him to feel again, something she'd thought she'd forgotten how to do. And he didn't have a billfold for a heart. She'd witnessed the actions of a kind, tender man, a man who hadn't left her side when she needed him, even though she was a stranger to him. A man who'd concerned himself with her son's health and who had, for whatever reason, chosen to pay all the hospital bills even though she didn't need him to.

It was that man she saw in her living room tonight. That man she was making love with. And to.

Her skin heated as she felt his lips lightly graze the outline of her ear and then the slope of her neck, the hollow of her throat.

Everything within her tightened with anticipation, moistened with desire. She had to keep reminding herself to breathe.

Like dry kindling, Sherry felt herself bursting in flame almost instantly.

She wanted this, needed this. Needed him, if only for the space of a night.

Live each moment as it comes, her mother had once said to her. It was never more true than now.

She threaded her arms around his neck, finding his mouth, kissing him hard, her body so close to his the glitter from her gown scattered itself along his tuxedo, branding it.

''Where's your bedroom?'' His voice was low, raspy against her ear.

It took effort to open her eyes. When she did, they sparkled with humor as she looked at him.

Had he said something funny? ''What?''

''A man who asks directions.'' She undid his tie. ''I like that.''

The feel of her cool fingers against his throat made his body temperature go up another notch. Desire urgently pulsed through his veins. ''That'll be the only direction I'll need.''

The promise stole her breath away. Again.

She turned from him toward the stairs. Raising the hem of her dress with one hand, she took his hand in the other and led the way up. She was surprised that her knees were still functioning. She could have sworn they'd melted away in the first encounter.

''This way.''

At the top of the stairs, as she passed her son's door, Sherry hesitated a fraction of a second.

''You want to look in on him?'' Sin-Jin asked. He saw the question in her eyes as she looked over her shoulder at him. He wasn't a mind reader, though there were some who'd accused him of that. ''I read body language, remember?''

Another man would have been in a hurry to get her to her room, to get her out of her clothes and make love with her, thinking only of himself. Sin-Jin had placed her needs ahead of his own.

He inched up a little further in her estimation.

She cracked the door to her son's room. Johnny was in his crib, lying on his back, soft, dark lashes just touching his cheeks. An angel sleeping peacefully.

Tranquility joined the host of emotions crowding within her.

Very softly Sherry closed the door again. She turned to look at Sin-Jin.

Who are you? she wondered for the hundredth time. "Thank you."

"Don't mention it." His smile crept under her skin, heating her down to the very core.

Her room was next to her son's, done all in whites, light grays and blues. Sin-Jin took note of his surroundings. Cool, yet somehow still warm. The room suited her.

The moment she was inside, he turned her around and kissed her again, softly, gently.

Something exploded inside of her. Suddenly Sherry felt like the aggressor, eager, desirous, unable to wait for that fulfilling moment, that final release that brought with it exhilaration and peace all at the same moment.

The instant his lips touched hers, an energy filled her, governing her moves. She started with his jacket, pushing it off his shoulders, stripping it from his arms. And then his shirt. Her hands felt as if they were trembling as she worked the buttons from their holes, moved the fabric from his skin.

His chest was lightly covered with dark hair. Excitement rose up another notch, mingling with sensuality that threatened to undo her completely.

He found her eagerness endearing and igniting. The fact that he wasn't mentally standing back, that he discovered himself to be as eager as she took him completely by surprise. For the first time in a very long while, he wasn't viewing what was going on in a controlled capacity. Instead he was in the midst of it, caught up in the moment, in the anticipation and the rising passion that seemed to be hammering at him.

Caught up in the woman.

He liked to affect people, liked to leave his imprint on their lives. Here it was almost as if the roles were reversed. She was doing something to him, stirring him in ways he, with his perfect ability to recall, couldn't remember ever having been stirred.

Stirred not shaken. Well, he was both and losing all sense of time, of place, of everything but the woman who'd done this to him.

Sliding the zipper of her dress down along the curve of her spine, Sin-Jin branded her with his mouth, his excitement increasing proportionately as the gown slowly slid from her body until it was finally on the floor, leaving her dressed in shimmering stockings that came up to her thighs, a tiny white thong and high heels.

He felt a tightness all through his body. It took everything he had not to take her at this moment. But he held himself in check. Wanting the moment to go on a little longer.

Sin-Jin forced himself to back away from her as his eyes skimmed over her body. She was even more sensational than he'd imagined. "You look like every pubescent boy's fantasy."

Her eyes held his, searching for something she needed to sustain her. "And what about your fantasy? What do I have to do to be that?"

"Just be," he whispered. The words glided along her skin like a sinful promise.

Everything drifted into a blurry haze for her after that, full of flash and fire and longing. Of sharp moments surrounding heightened reactions. Each sensation took her a little farther, a little higher up the path that led to the final plateau.

She never knew she could feel like this, it was like being in the middle of a tempest, and she was both afraid and exhilarated at what was happening to her. At what was coming.

It was the difference between a song and a symphony, Sin-Jin realized as he felt her eager lips skimming along his throat, his chest.

His body hummed with suppressed urges as their nude bodies tangled on the bed, generating heat, slick with desire still unspent.

Moving over her, he threaded his hands through her hair, but rather than enter her, Sin-Jin kissed her over and over again, assaulting her mouth, her neck, the swell of her breasts, her very being.

Feeling her twist and quiver beneath him was almost more than he could resist, her hips arching in an unspoken, urgent invitation. But suddenly, for reasons he couldn't quite crystallize, it was important to him to turn this night into something memorable for her.

And to somehow get his fill of her, though he was beginning to feel that it was impossible.

When he finally drove himself into her, the sensation was all powerful for him. The dance was short, fiery and intense. And when it was over, when he rolled off her and onto his back, completely spent, he thought he was seriously in danger of never being able to catch his breath again.

Sin-Jin waited for his usual waning of interest, of desire; the feeling that always came as a prelude to his moving on.

It didn't come.

There was no hollow feeling, no widening hole within his being. No desire to get up and leave as quickly as possible.

All he wanted to do was hold her closer. And so he did, telling himself to be patient. She'd aroused more passion within him than any woman ever had, it was only natural that the inevitable might take a little longer to appear.

For now he could drift within this false feeling of contentment.

Sin-Jin gazed at her, wondering who this innocent-looking woman who had just rocked his world was.

His breathing only now was becoming more steady. "Are you all right?"

Her smile was dreamy, pulling him in again. If he'd had the energy, he would have been surprised.

"I'll let you know once I find out if I still have a pulse left."

Concern nudged itself forward. "Was it too soon for you?" he asked.

"I believe Goldilocks had a phrase for it." Sherry

turned her face up to his and smiled. "It was 'just right.'"

He kissed the top of her head. "So is that who you are? Goldilocks?"

"Right now, if you were to interrogate me, I couldn't even give you my name, rank and serial number." Sherry raised herself up on her elbow and looked at him, her breasts teasing his skin as she moved. "Who *was* that masked man?"

Sin-Jin laughed as the contentment he didn't want to place stock in spread out a little farther within him. "If you're trying to flatter me, you've succeeded."

"I'm not trying to flatter you, I'm just trying to figure out if I was in an earthquake or a time warp." She fell back against the pillow, her hair fanning out about her like a reddish cloud. She sighed deeply. "Wow. If you raid corporations the way you make love, the world might as well give up and make you emperor now. All hail, Emperor Sin-Jin."

She was completely guileless. Was that possible for a woman? And a reporter at that? He didn't know. All he knew was that he was being reeled in and damn if he wasn't enjoying it.

Sin-Jin tucked her closer to him. "You weren't exactly shabby yourself."

She pretended to take offense. "Oh, well, that's terrific. Is that it? That's what they'll put on my tombstone? 'She wasn't shabby herself'?"

"Fantastic, all right?" He kissed her temples one at a time, arousing himself as he did so. "You were fantastic." He kissed each eyelid in turn, feeling himself begin to surge. "And besides, it's far too soon to talk of tombstones."

She sighed, weaving her arms around his neck. "Make love to me like that again and it might not be too soon at all."

He smiled into her soul, feeling his own catch fire again. "Is that an invitation?"

She rubbed against him enticingly. "Do you want it to be?"

The woman really was a siren. But for now, he assured himself, he knew just where the rocks were, and he wasn't about to be dashed against any of them. "Questions, always questions. I guess I'll have to stop you the way I did last time."

She turned toward him, her body pressing against his. She felt his response and smiled wickedly. "I was hoping you'd say that."

The crying woke him.

When Sin-Jin opened his eyes, the unfamiliarity of his surroundings momentarily disoriented him. He was in Sherry's bedroom. The sound that had roused him was coming from the baby monitor next to the far side of the bed.

He hadn't realized that he'd fallen asleep.

Raising himself up on his elbows, he realized that what he was hearing was Johnny crying. The place beside him was empty. He skimmed his hand over it. It was still warm. A small rush undulated through him. He swept it away before it could complete its route.

Sin-Jin sat up and dragged his hand through his hair. He glanced at his wristwatch. It was almost four in the morning. Well past time to get going. He reached for his underwear and then his trousers. As he pulled them on, he thought about getting dressed and simply slipping out the front door. That way he could avoid the necessity for having to engage in any awkward conversation with Sherry. It seemed like the thing to do.

The trouble was, he didn't want to leave, didn't want to simply vanish into the darkness, like Batman.

He wanted to stay.

To see her with her child.

What the hell was happening to him?

The next moment, he shrugged. What was the harm in remaining for a few minutes, he upbraided himself. He was overreacting. All he was planning to do was be polite and say goodbye, not promise her half the kingdom.

The crying stopped. A soft, contented noise followed in its wake.

Curious, Sin-Jin tiptoed to the doorway of the next room in his bare feet.

The nursery smelled faintly of talcum powder and of the soft, seductive scent of her cologne.

Moonlight streamed in through the window, slipping through the white nylon curtains and bathing parts of the room. Half in shadow, half in light, Sherry was sitting in a rocking chair next to the crib, holding her son in her arms and rocking ever so slightly. The infant was sucking madly on the bottle she held to his mouth.

Sin-Jin stood in the doorway, just watching them for the space of a moment. Wondering why such a simple thing could move him so much.

Maybe it was the love he felt, the love that was

so evident between the mother and the child she held in her arms.

Sherry sensed his presence before she looked toward the doorway.

''Hi,'' she said softly. Even in the dim light of the moon, she looked radiant to him. ''I'm sorry, did we wake you?''

We. As if whatever her son did was an action that she gladly shared, gladly took responsibility for. He felt envious of the baby, envious of the life that was yet to unfold before him. John Campbell was never going to lack for love, never feel that he was alone in the world.

Sin-Jin half shrugged, feeling suddenly as if he was intruding. ''I heard crying.''

''He was hungry.'' She smiled down at the little soul in her arms. ''Actually, I'm surprised he didn't wake up sooner. He was giving me a break. I guess he knew tonight was special.'' She raised her eyes to Sin-Jin's face. ''We don't usually have overnight guests.''

He knew what she was saying without her stating it outright. That she didn't do this casually. That she didn't just top off the evening by taking someone to her bed.

She didn't have to tell him. He knew. God only knew how he knew, but he knew.

What the hell was he doing here standing half-dressed, barefoot in a child's nursery, watching a scene out of a Norman Rockwell calendar? This wasn't the place for him. He shifted uncomfortably. ''I should be going.''

She wanted to ask him not to, but that would be

needy, and she wasn't about to let him think that she was the clingy sort. She knew it was wrong to hope, yet everything within her wanted him to stay, just a little while longer. To let her pretend, just a few more minutes.

"I know." When, to her surprise, Sin-Jin made no move to leave, she stopped rocking. "Would you like to feed him for a while?"

Sin-Jin unconsciously pressed his lips together. *Go, damn it. Get out of here. This isn't for you.*

"I—"

The very fact that he didn't say no, that he hesitated, gave Sherry her answer. She rose to her feet, the folds of her robe barely slipping closed.

"It's easy. Here, just hold him against you in the crook of your arm." Before he could protest that he really needed to be going, she made the transfer. "And sit down in the rocker. If you hold the bottle anywhere near his mouth, Johnny'll do the rest."

Sin-Jin did as she instructed, and the infant continued sucking on his bottle. He couldn't explain the warm feeling that originated at the point of contact between himself and the child, nor why it spread outward so quickly. Couldn't explain it and didn't want to try. It was too early in the morning to contemplate complex matters.

He just rocked and enjoyed the moment.

Chapter Thirteen

Hints of twilight found their way through the wide bay windows of the twentieth floor of Adair Industries. This reminded Sin-Jin that it was getting late.

Within the room were sixteen of his finest people, all seated around the perimeter of the highly polished teak oval conference table he'd picked up in the Philippines on his last business junket there.

To his left was Mrs. Farley, dutifully taking down every word being uttered. On his right, appropriately enough, was Carver Jackson, his right-hand man for the past five years. Carver had come to him straight out of Harvard Business School, clutching his MBA and eager to set the world on fire. He'd never found the younger man wanting in any way.

But right now he found himself wanting. Wanting to be somewhere else other than here. It was the tail end of an excellent week that had seen significant corporate gains for Adair Industries. For once he was satisfied. It was a new experience for him.

Of late he'd found himself experiencing a great many new sensations.

There was a pregnant pause as Althea Mayfair had just finished her report. He'd hardly kept his mind on the words, but knew that her work was miles beyond competent, as was Althea.

Splaying his hands on either side, he leaned forward and looked at the faces of each and every one of them. "Go home, people."

Carver's thin brows furrowed over his hawklike nose. Startled, he glanced at his watch and then exchanged looks with Edna Farley. They'd hardly begun to dig in.

"But it's not even a school night, boss." The cryptic smile on Carver's lips gave way to a sobered look. "What gives?"

Under the watchful eyes of everyone present, Sin-Jin began returning various folders and disks to his titanium briefcase. "I thought for once everyone would like to get home before eight."

It was only five o'clock. Carver looked a little unnerved. Was this a joke? "If this is your idea of a production of *A Christmas Carol,* you're several months early."

Rather than begin dispersing, everyone around the table appeared to be sealed to their seats, their eyes trained on Sin-Jin.

A whimsical smile found its way to his lips. "This is not a test. I repeat, this is not a test, it's a genuine order. Go home."

No one moved except Carver, who rose to his feet to peer more closely at Sin-Jin's face. "Are you feeling all right, sir?"

If he felt any better, Sin-Jin realized, it might actually be illegal. "I'm feeling fine, why?"

Carver shook his head, glancing around at the others at the table. To a one, they seemed stunned. "This isn't like you."

No, it wasn't, and maybe that was the shame of it, Sin-Jin thought. "I've decided that maybe there're more important things in the world than the next corporate takeover."

Shaken, Carver looked to Sin-Jin's secretary for guidance, but the woman appeared to be unaffected by what was going on. She was even smiling. "Now I know you're not feeling well."

Rather than answer, Sin-Jin looked to the woman he'd always felt was the only one who truly understood him. It was through her that he directed his money to the various charities that he supported. He could trust Mrs. Farley to safely keep his largess a secret. She was the only one left alive, aside from his estranged parents, who knew him when.

"Mrs. Farley, help me out here."

Rising to her feet, the prim woman looked at Carver, waved her hand in a classic motion of dismissal and said, "Shoo."

Nervous laughter echoed in the room.

Carver attempted to make light of the situation, wondering if a call to 911 was necessary. "Well, I guess that settles it. Science has finally managed to clone an adult. How do we get ahold of the company?"

Sin-Jin snapped his briefcase shut. "You can put that on the agenda for Monday, no, Tuesday," he corrected himself.

Wanting in on what he assumed had to be some kind of a joke, Carver asked, "What happened to Monday?"

"It was swallowed up in a three-day weekend, Carver." Sin-Jin told him matter-of-factly. "Look at your calendar."

Carver frowned. This was becoming stranger and stranger. Several people slowly began getting their things together, all still watching Sin-Jin for any indication that this was some kind of strange prank. "We've never taken a three-day weekend."

They were a good crew, loyal to a fault. And he'd robbed them of half their lives. It was time they began having lives outside of the corporation.

"We are now." He looked at the group, sixteen of the hardest workers he had the pleasure of knowing. "Go home," he repeated for a third time.

This time the order seemed to take. Papers rustled as they were packed away in briefcases that were already crammed full of files. Cases snapped, chairs moved silently along the rug as they were pushed back.

"See you Monday, boss," Althea called out.

"Tuesday," Sin-Jin reminded her as he walked quickly out the door.

With Sin-Jin gone, the conference room emptied out in a matter of minutes. Carver remained the only holdout. He turned toward Sin-Jin's secretary as she neatly gathered her things together. Something was definitely up, and she was the only one who would know what it was.

''Mrs. Farley, just what's happened to our fearless leader?''

She smiled. ''I believe *Love Finds Andy Hardy.*''

The response seemed to confuse Carver. ''Isn't that an old Mickey Rooney movie?''

A smile entered her eyes as she nodded. ''Among other things.''

''Who, what, where, when, how?''

''All good things a reporter would ask.'' She looked at him. ''But you're not a reporter.''

Carver stood in the room, alone now, thinking. And then it seemed to hit him.

''But she is,'' he called out.

Hearing him, Mrs. Farley continued walking down the hallway, neither confirming or denying. Had Carver been able to see her, however, he would have seen the smile on her face and had his answer.

She'd spent part of her day on the computer and part of it on the telephone. Spurred on by personal curiosity rather than her original assignment, she'd discovered that trying to track down Sin-Jin's origins only brought her to a blank wall over and over again. He seemed to have no history until he came on the scene to spearhead a takeover of what was to become Adair Industries. Frustrated, she'd done a search on John Fletcher, thinking that if she could locate the man, maybe he would provide, however inadvertently, a few answers for her. Or at least a clue.

The cabin at Wrightwood was indeed in John

Fletcher's name. The only trouble was, the address given as a permanent residence turned out to belong to a plot in Los Angeles that had long since been abandoned.

The rest of her search was equally as frustrating. The country, it turned out, had a host of John Fletchers and she was patiently trying to weed her way through them. She kept at it until four o'clock.

Temporarily giving up the quest, she turned her attention to the night that lay ahead. It was time to get ready.

Sin-Jin took the turn a little faster than he should have and cautioned himself to go slower. Five minutes weren't going to make a difference. It wasn't as if she was going to disappear if he wasn't on her doorstep at exactly the appointed time.

Carver was right, he was behaving strangely.

He didn't want to think about it, or even acknowledge what was happening, but anyone who knew him would have said that he was undergoing a transformation. He could see the amusement in Mrs. Farley's eyes when he caught her looking at him. She knew, he thought. But then, she had always been intuitive.

For the first time he was allowing his feelings to govern his actions. Why else would he have placed his private life above his corporate one? The meeting he'd abruptly brought to a close had been set to continue into the wee hours of the morning. They'd been brainstorming another corporate takeover. This time it was a failing movie studio that had overextended itself in the last few years. He had ideas, a whole spectrum of ideas on how to improve operations, trim away the fat, get the hundred-year-old enterprise back on its feet again and begin earning a profit by the end of the next fiscal year.

It wasn't for lack of ideas that he'd terminated the meeting.

But amid all these ideas that were percolating in his brain, images of Sherry kept finding their way into his mind. Sherry, the way she'd been the last time they'd made love. The way she would be the next time he held her in his arms. It made it hard for a man to think about anything but the woman who was consuming him.

He was falling into a trap and he knew it.

But knowing didn't help. He was still standing willingly within the circle of iron teeth set to spring.

Like an alcoholic in denial, Sin-Jin told himself that he could walk away anytime, close the door on what he was feeling at any given moment. Denial allowed him to believe that lingering here like this was all right.

What was the harm in enjoying himself? he argued as he drove down what had become a familiar street to him.

Sherry made him laugh, she made him feel good, and he was careful not to say things to her that he would regret the next day. Things that had to do with emotions, that had to do with his past.

As long as he remembered the rules, everything could go on the way it was a little while longer.

Stopping at home for a quick change of clothing, he pulled his Mercedes up into her driveway a shade before seven. He was dressed in semiformal evening wear. Mrs. Farley had made the reservations at the exclusive restaurant for eight. It gave them enough time to get there even in the height of traffic.

As he walked to Sherry's front door, it occurred to him that he didn't see her mother's car in the vicinity. She was supposed to baby-sit.

Had the Campbells come by and taken the baby with them instead? He'd been looking forward to seeing the little boy.

A warning signal went off in his head. He was displaying all the signs of a man who was getting attached to not only a woman but to her child. He was going to have to watch that.

When he rang the doorbell, she opened it almost instantly. Barefoot, she was wearing a tank top that casually flirted with the waistband of her jeans, showing off a stomach that had become flat in an incredibly short amount of time. There was what appeared to be a dab of some kind of tomato sauce on the kitchen towel she had slung over her shoulder.

She was usually very punctual. Was something wrong? ''You're not dressed.''

Sherry spread her hands and looked down at herself. ''I'm not naked.''

He'd be lying if he denied that part of him wished she was. ''No, I mean for the restaurant. Did I get the night wrong?'' The question was merely to be polite. He never got any date wrong.

Taking his arm, Sherry drew him into the house. ''No, but I decided that instead of going out, I'd treat you to a home-cooked meal.''

He glanced over his shoulder as the door closed. ''I didn't see your mother's car outside.''

"My home, my meal," she emphasized. "I can cook, you know."

It wasn't her cooking that interested him about her. "Why bother?"

"Because it's more intimate."

He followed her into the kitchen. There were pots simmering on the stove and all sorts of things going on on the counters. He was beginning to realize that she did nothing halfheartedly. "I didn't think we could get more intimate."

"Maybe not our bodies," she agreed, stirring the pot of sauce. "But our souls, well, that could stand a little more work."

He didn't quite follow the transition. "And that'll be accomplished by you cooking for me?"

He didn't understand, she thought. She wanted to do these things for him. It seemed somehow more real than walking into a restaurant to eat food someone else had prepared, leave dishes that someone else had to wash. "Now who's questioning everything? Open that bottle of wine for me."

"Must be the company I keep." He picked up the corkscrew she pointed to and worked it into the cork, pulling it out.

She paused to kiss him. "Must be."

Sin-Jin ran his tongue over his lips. "Mmm, what is that?"

She was already turning back to the stove. "Me, I hope."

Running his tongue over his lips again, he tried to place the taste. "Not unless your lips have suddenly gotten spicy."

"I was sampling my tomato sauce." Some of the

sauce must have remained on her lips. "I think something's missing."

In reply, he turned her around and swept her into his arms. Sin-Jin kissed her again, longer this time, then pretended to taste his lips again. "Not a damn thing that I can think of."

She laughed. "You're supposed to eat the sauce off a plate, not my lips."

Pouring a glass of red wine for her, he placed it on the counter next to her, then poured one for himself. "To each his own." He leaned over and went to kiss her again.

She stopped him with a hand to his chest. "Later," she said, staving him off. "That's after dessert."

The look in his eyes was sensuously wicked. "That *is* dessert."

"You know," she said, her voice softening, "sometimes you can be awfully nice."

He paused to take a drink of his wine, then removed his jacket. It was hot in the kitchen. "Not too many people would agree with you."

She sniffed. "Then not too many people know the real you."

He came up behind her, unable to resist. Threading his arms around her waist, Sin-Jin nuzzled her neck. "Do you?"

Her eyes threatened to flutter shut. It took effort to concentrate on the meal she was making. "I'm working on it."

Kissing her neck, he released her and backed up. The least he could do, when she was going through all this effort, was not to get in her way.

He took another sip of wine, then leaned a hip against the counter and watched her work. "I let everyone go home early today."

Breaking up spaghetti and dropping it into the boiling pot, she smiled to herself, thinking of how that must have come across. "I bet that was a shock to them."

He laughed, remembering the looks on everyone's faces. "I practically had to shove them out the door."

"You've trained them well." Stirring the spaghetti to keep it from clumping together, she glanced in his direction. "I imagine they're all very loyal to you."

Was that the woman he'd made love with asking, or the reporter? "Is that off the record?"

She could almost read his thoughts. "I'm not a reporter tonight, Sin-Jin, and you're not the great corporate raider. We're just two people about to enjoy a home-cooked meal, a store-bought dessert—" her eyes glinted with humor "—and lots of red-hot loving after it's over." She cocked her head, looking at his expression. He wasn't the easiest man to read. Was she saying too much? Or not enough? "Or should I call it sex?"

The one was too hot, the other too cold. "Why label it at all?"

She found herself wanting answers and knowing that she shouldn't. If she squeezed too hard, what she held in her hand would slip away. "I thought you were the one who liked to have everything neatly labeled and placed in a niche."

He was. Until now. If he put a name to it, if he defined what was going on between them, he'd have to go. And he didn't want to. "Some things defy labeling."

Everything on the stove was going according to plan. She let the pots fend for themselves for the moment and crossed to him. "Like me?"

He smiled, caressing her face. Was it him, or did she just keep getting more beautiful every time he saw her? "Like you."

It took effort not to sigh with contentment. "I'll take that as a compliment."

"It was meant as one." He was more in danger of boiling over than the pot of spaghetti. Taking a breath, he backed off. "So, what else would you like me to do besides open up the bottle of wine?"

Everything was almost ready. She had a little time. "You could try priming the cook a little more."

He set his glass of wine on the counter beside hers. "And just how do I do that?"

"You're a very intelligent man." Her eyes smiled up into his. "You figure it out."

Sin-Jin took her into his arms. "How's this?"

The smile spread from her eyes to her lips. "Keep going, you're on the right trail."

Was he? he wondered as he kissed her. Or was he going deeper and deeper into the woods, about to get as lost as his father and mother always had.

For now, Sin-Jin shut his mind down and let his emotions take over. There was time enough later to sort it all out.

"You know, I was also planning on taking you dancing." Rinsing off another dish, he handed it to her. Sherry placed it into the dishwasher.

That was the last of them. After shutting the dishwasher door, she switched it on. It hummed to life. Sherry stepped away from the appliance, raising her voice to be heard about the noise. "You sound as if that's not possible anymore."

It was still early enough to go out, but there was another obstacle. "Don't you have to get a sitter for the baby?"

"Why?" Her look was innocent, teasing.

She was up to something, but he played along. "Well, we're not about to go out and leave Johnny alone."

"We're not about to go out at all," she informed him mysteriously.

"But didn't you just say—"

He was really so straitlaced, she loved teasing him. "I said we can still go dancing. It's only as far away as the next source of music. Unless, of course, you're one of those people who dances to some inner tune he hears."

He shook his head. "The only thing I hear is you."

"We can change that."

Taking hold of his hand, Sherry drew Sin-Jin into the living room. She'd had this in mind all along. Everything had already been prepared before he arrived.

She pressed a button on her home entertainment unit and the air was suddenly filled with soft, bluesy music. Turning around, she presented herself to him. "You can ask me to dance now."

He laughed, inclining his head. "May I have this dance?"

She affected a Southern drawl as she fanned herself and fluttered her lashes. "Well, I seem to have this space open on my dance card, sir, so I suppose it'll be all right just this once, even if you did wait till the last minute to ask."

Taking her hand in his, he pressed his other hand to the small of her back and began to dance to the slow song. "You're crazy, you know that?"

"There's been some talk," she allowed, still in character, "but I don't pay them no mind."

Looking up at him, their eyes met for a moment, and things were said silently that could not be said aloud. Smiling, she laid her head against his shoulder and let her mind drift away with the music.

"This is nice," he said, his breath tingling the back of her neck.

She looked up at him, her heart swelling. "Yes, I know."

Sin-Jin stopped dancing and kissed her.

He stayed the night, as she knew he would. Just as he had the other nights that he had come to take her out. And when the lovemaking was over and she lay beside him in the dark, she listened to his even breathing and thought about things.

In a distant corner of her mind, she knew she was playing with fire, allowing herself to feel things for a man who might be out of her life tomorrow, or if not tomorrow, then the day after. But it was as if she had no say in the matter. Things were happening inside her that were beyond her control.

Everything was finite and an end was coming.

Knowing that it was didn't prepare her any more than lecturing to herself did.

So for the time being, she went on pretending that she was just another woman who was falling in love and that he was just another man, knowing that both were false.

Chapter Fourteen

"For a generous man, you certainly are hard to find, John Fletcher," Sherry murmured.

She was sitting in her home office, frowning at her computer screen. Several feet away from her, Johnny was quietly sleeping in the bassinet that Owen had given her. Johnny had turned out to be the best baby ever, sleeping long periods of time and waking with a sunny disposition, but right now her mind wasn't on her son. It was on the mystery stacked up before her.

She had on her desk documentation of the charitable contributions that John Fletcher had made over the past nine years. Even without resorting to a calculator, she could see that they came to quite an overwhelming sum. Whoever this John Fletcher was, he was obviously generous to a fault. Someone like that would need to keep his identity a secret to prevent the onslaught of everyone with a hard-luck story.

Confounded by what she wasn't finding on the computer, Sherry leafed through the contributions, looking for a clue, something to go on that would take her farther than nowhere.

Was it some kind of a coincidence that the contributions began one year from the day that Sin-Jin had emerged to take over and rename Adair Industries? Or that the checks made to the charities all passed through the same bank that handled both the Adair Industries accounts and Sin-Jin's private ones?

This would lead someone to believe that John Fletcher was somehow connected to Adair Industries, especially since Sin-Jin had been using the man's cabin that fateful weekend she'd given birth to Johnny.

But if there was a connection, where was the man? It was as if he was in hiding. There were no payroll checks made out to him and no history of his ever having worked for Adair Industries in any capacity. Except for his deep pockets and his cabin, he was, for all intents and purposes, an invisible man.

Because of his connection to Sin-Jin and because of the timing of that first check, she arbitrarily placed the phantom man in an age range approximately five years younger to five years older than Sin-Jin and had begun her search there. With the aid of Rusty's friend, she tapped into restricted databases, wading through social security files of men with that name born in that particular decade.

Weeding through the various John Fletchers one

by one was a tedious process that led her to premature obituaries, improbable locations, county jails and dead ends that defied breaching.

The men she actually did locate just didn't fit the profile. After talking to them or their spouses for a few minutes, Sherry instinctively knew she'd come across yet another wrong John Fletcher.

She sat back in her chair, sipping coffee that had long since grown cold and trying to piece together what she had so far—which was next to nothing.

So who the hell was he? she thought in utter frustration.

Johnny began to stir. ''Motherhood first,'' she announced to no one and went to see to her son.

He needed changing, feeding and a little bonding. So did she, she thought. Sin-Jin was out of town for the day and wouldn't be back until morning. She tried not to miss him too much. And tried not to feel too guilty over what she was doing.

Since it was late, she put Johnny down for what she hoped was a good part of the night and then came downstairs to shut down her computer. On a whim, promising herself that this was the last one she was going to try, she keyed in John Fletcher and searched through the Nevada phone books. There was none. It didn't surprise her. But when she went to the birth and death records, she discovered that there had been a John Fletcher born in the Lake Tahoe region.

As Sherry remembered a panoramic framed photograph of the Lake Tahoe region on the mantel of Fletcher's cabin, excitement began to hum through her.

Scanning the death records, she found nothing.

Working forward from his birth, she couldn't find any record of him after the age of eighteen. Nothing at all. It was as if the earth had just swallowed him up. She knew how many homicides went unsolved each year, how many missing persons were destined to remain that way forever. She might never be able to find this particular John Fletcher. She told herself to let it go.

But if this John Fletcher had no history after eighteen, where were the checks coming from? He *had* to be the right John Fletcher.

She was getting punchy, she thought, but she had nothing else, and something in her gut told her she might be on to something. At the very least, it gave her something to explore.

Adrenaline was pumping through her veins. Ignoring the fact that it was getting late, she reached for the telephone and dialed her parents.

Her mother answered on the third ring, just before the answering machine kicked in.

"Mom, it's Sherry—"

"Well, of course it is, dear. No one else calls me Mom."

"Right." She tried not to sound impatient. "Would you mind staying with Johnny for the day tomorrow?"

Sheila laughed. "That's like asking a chocoholic if they'd mind visiting Hershey, PA. Of course I wouldn't mind. Why?" Her tone ripened with interest. "Is Sin-Jin taking you somewhere?"

Sherry smiled enigmatically to herself as she looked at the information on the computer monitor. "In a manner of speaking."

* * *

After boarding an early-morning plane for the Lake Tahoe region and renting a car, Sherry had driven to the town she'd discovered yesterday—Hathaway, Nevada. Because nothing else occurred to her, she began with the high schools. There were three in the area and she'd struck out with two of them.

Paydirt came with the third.

The woman sitting behind the desk that guarded the principal's office had informed her that Dr. Grace Rafferty was out of town, not due back until the following week. Desperate, Sherry had played a long shot, giving her credentials and telling the woman she was attempting to find a John Fletcher. The woman's face had lit up immediately. ''That delightful young man just sent the school a handsome bequest. And when Dr. Rafferty offered to draw up a petition to have the school named after him, he declined. Imagine that.''

Money. The key that tied everything together. He *had* to be the right John Fletcher. She needed to nurture this along. The woman, she decided, looked old enough to have been here when Fletcher graduated. ''By any chance, do you remember John Fletcher?''

The woman's features softened considerably. ''Why, yes, I remember John Fletcher. Outstanding student. Outstanding. But very quiet. Kept to himself a great deal.'' She shook her head. ''Not a thing like his parents.''

Sherry almost felt giddy. She was actually finally

getting somewhere. ''His parents?'' It was hard to curb her eagerness. ''Are they still alive?''

The woman, Mrs. Sellers, considered the question. ''I imagine so. They're long gone from the area, of course. Given their lifestyles, they were hardly ever here at all, even when they did live here.''

Sherry could feel her lead slipping through her fingers. ''But you made it sound as if John was a student here for a longer period of time.''

''He was. Times were that he was the only one in the house, aside from the servants, of course. If you ask me,'' the woman confided, lowering her voice, ''they were the ones who raised him, not his parents. They were in and out of his life like tourists on a holiday. I strongly suspect the only one who had a lasting effect on John Fletcher was Mrs. Farley.''

Sherry felt as if she'd just opened a door that led to *The Twilight Zone*. It seemed like just too much of a coincidence. ''Who?''

''Mrs. Farley. Edna Farley. Finest English teacher we ever had.'' The woman leaned forward confidentially. ''Not like this new crop we've been getting.'' The woman looked genuinely saddened as she added, ''Mrs. Farley retired several years ago.''

Sherry felt her heartbeat accelerating. ''Do you have a picture of Mrs. Farley?''

Mrs. Sellers looked at her as if she was slightly simple. ''In our yearbooks, of course.''

The yearbook. Adrenaline kicked up another notch, hummed a John Philip Sousa march. ''What year did John Fletcher graduate?''

''Give me a minute.'' Moving her chair back, she began typing on her keyboard. One screen after another opened on the monitor as she hit the appropriate keys. "There." Turning the monitor so that Sherry could see for herself, she indicated the line in question.

That would make him Sin-Jin's age. Sherry tried not to sound as excited as she felt. "May I see that year's yearbook, please?"

"Yes, of course." The woman rose from her desk. She was almost tiny in stature. Mrs. Sellers pushed up the sleeves of her sweater. "It might take me some time to find it."

The search through the bookshelves in the back of the office was shorter than Sherry expected. Mrs. Sellers triumphantly placed the volume in question before Sherry on the small desk.

"Senior photos are generally in the middle." The telephone rang. Torn, the woman had no choice but to return to her desk, leaving Sherry alone with the yearbook.

Sherry looked down at her hands. They were shaking as she flipped to the middle of the yearbook. Taking a deep breath, she found the *F*s.

Scanning one page, she found what she was looking for at the top of the other.

Her breath caught in her throat.

John Fletcher could have been Sin-Jin's younger brother.

Or Sin-Jin at eighteen.

Hoping against hope, she flipped to the front of the section, to the *A*s, but there was no St. John Adair graduating that year.

She closed the book.

"Find him?" Mrs. Sellers asked.

Sherry rose and crossed to the woman. "Yes, I did. I was wondering, could you look through your database and see if there was ever a student here by the name of St. John Adair? *A-d-a-i-r.* He would have graduated at approximately the same time."

Mrs. Sellers typed the name in, then shook her head. "I'm afraid we've never had a student by that name."

Yes you did, but his name was Fletcher then. "I didn't think so," Sherry murmured for form's sake. She looked down at the leather-bound book in her hands. "You said there were photographs of the teaching staff in the yearbooks."

"Right here." Taking the book from her, Mrs. Sellers flipped it open to the front and found the right section. She pointed to a black-and-white photograph. "There she is. Edna Farley."

It was Sin-Jin's Mrs. Farley.

She didn't understand.

It was obvious that Sin-Jin had changed his name, that he was this mysterious John Fletcher, but to what end? As far as she could discern after spending the day here, there were no skeletons in his closet, no unsolved crimes or murders in the town that could somehow be traced to him or to his parents. Why all the secrecy?

She'd remained in the town the entire afternoon. Mrs. Sellers gave her directions to the Fletcher house, or rather, the Fletcher estate.

Located on the outskirts of town, the building could have been taken for a small castle in centuries gone by. It actually had been one once. Sin-Jin's mother had fallen in love with it on her honeymoon and his father had had it transported to the United States where it was rebuilt, stone by stone. It turned out to be the most solid thing about their lives.

Victoria and William Fletcher were the epitome of a mismatched couple. They had little in common other than a love of the finer things in life and partying. Eventually, they divorced and moved on to marry others. Many others. Both products of wealthy families, John Fletcher's parents had no vocations, no goals in life other than enjoyment. She couldn't help wondering where Sin-Jin had fitted in all this.

No wonder he'd taken so readily to her mother and father, she thought. Who wouldn't after having these two as parents?

The pair were obviously self-involved flakes, she thought as she took the commuter flight back to John Wayne Airport. Her heart ached for him, for the boy Sin-Jin had once been, living alone in that cold, gray castle.

Was he ashamed of his parents, was that why he kept his past a secret?

As the plane taxied down on the runway some forty-five minutes later, Sherry discovered that she had far more questions now than when she had first taken off for Tahoe this morning.

Weary, confused and still feeling marginally guilty about what she was doing, Sherry wasn't prepared to see Sin-Jin's black Mercedes parked at her curb as she drove up to her house.

Her pulse began to race. Would he be able to tell

what she'd found out? She angled her rearview mirror as she came to a stop. Was it there on her face?

She turned off the ignition. The professional thing would be to confront him, but she didn't feel very professional right now. Just confused.

Love did that to a person, she realized as she got out of the car and walked up to her front door.

"There she is." Sitting on the sofa next to Sin-Jin, Sheila twisted around to see her daughter walking in. She smiled a greeting.

Sin-Jin rose to his feet. Sherry saw a hint of concern in his eyes. Did he suspect where she'd been? He crossed to her, kissing her lightly.

"Hi, I tried to call you earlier, and your mother said you'd gone out."

She cleared her throat, offering up a smile. Damn it, you'd think an investigative reporter would be better at keeping cool under duress. "I had."

He heard the evasiveness in her voice. His eyebrows narrowed slightly as he studied her face. "Where did you go?"

Desperation bred the lie. She wasn't ready to tell him that she knew who he really was. Because she wasn't ready to see him walk away.

"I got together with the ladies of The Mom Squad." She'd mentioned the group to him before and crossed her fingers that none of the women had seen fit to call her today. She glanced at her mother, but there was nothing in the other woman's face to indicate that she suspected her daughter was lying. "Lori's definitely beginning to show and I think that Joanna looks like she's going to pop any second." Given that the women had looked this way a week ago, she figured she was safe in making the comment to Sin-Jin.

"Are they coming to the christening?" Sheila asked.

Sherry nodded, making a mental note to caution the women not to say anything about not having seen her today. She sighed inwardly. This was getting complicated. "They wouldn't miss it." She turned to Sin-Jin. "How about you? Are you still coming?"

He found that he was actually looking forward to the experience. "I cleared my calendar."

"Johnny will be honored."

Even as she said the name, Sherry was suddenly struck by the irony of the situation. Inadvertently, without knowing it, she actually *had* named her son after the man who had delivered him. That was why Sin-Jin had looked so surprised when she'd told him her baby's name. He'd probably thought that she had somehow stumbled onto the truth.

She still didn't understand why he'd done what he'd done, only that he had.

Sheila picked up her purse and sweater from the sofa. "Well, I'll leave you two to do whatever."

"Mom—" There was a warning note in Sherry's voice.

Sheila was the soul of innocence. "I wasn't being specific, was I, Sin-Jin? 'Whatever' covers a huge range of things." Passing him, Sheila patted him on his arm. "See you at the church."

"Church?" he echoed, looking from the woman who'd just walked out to the one beside him.

"The christening, remember?" Sherry laughed. She kicked off her shoes. "You look like someone who's just seen a ghost. If you think she was saying something about weddings and marriage, that was far too subtle for my mother."

"I'm beginning to see that." Moving her shoes out of the way, he sat down on the sofa again, making himself at home. "I like your mother." He took her hand, pulling her toward him. "Your father, too."

Sherry slipped onto his lap, getting comfortable. "That's good, because they like you."

And so do I. That's what makes this all so hard, Sin-Jin.

Guilt nibbled away at her. She felt somehow disloyal by probing into his life this way, and yet it was her job. Owen wouldn't fire her if she didn't come through; they had too much history together. But she would be disappointed in herself if she dropped the story. Letting her feelings dictate what she did or didn't write would set a precedent, one she didn't think she could live with.

But could she live with hurting Sin-Jin? He obviously didn't want people knowing about his past, and here she was, debating exposing it in exchange for her own byline. It felt like a lose-lose situation.

Sin-Jin brushed back her hair from her face, catching her attention. "A penny for your thoughts."

"Hmm?"

"A penny for your thoughts," he repeated. He laced his hands together around her. "You look as if you were a million miles away."

"A penny, huh?" She laughed, threading her arms around his neck. "Boy, now I know how you got so wealthy. You pay rock-bottom prices for everything.''

He looked at her, his eyes growing serious. ''Not always.''

He certainly wasn't paying rock-bottom prices for getting involved with her. It was going to require the ultimate price eventually. No matter how you dressed up the scenario, he was certain that it would end the way all his parents' liaisons and marriages had: with bitter feelings all around.

Damn it, he'd sworn to himself that it wouldn't happen to him, that he was above those kinds of needs, and here he was, up to his forehead in the very same thing. And still not willing to walk away while he still could.

He still could, couldn't he? he thought, framing her face with his hands.

He'd never been less sure of anything in his life, not even when he'd turned his back on his former life and just walked away. The only time he'd returned to the town where he'd grown up was when he'd heard about Mrs. Farley taking an early retirement from the school district. He'd flown back for her party, waited until it was over and then approached her with his proposition. She'd come to work for him the following Monday.

But except for that, he'd never gone home again.

No, it wasn't home, he amended, it had been a place where he'd grown up. Sherry's house was more home to him than that place, that castle, had ever been.

Sherry was home.

The concept scared the hell out of him.

"Okay, my turn."

Her voice drifted into his thoughts, mercifully pushing them aside. He looked at her. "Your turn for what?"

"To offer you a rock-bottom price for your thoughts. I'll even make it two pennies." There was something in his eyes, something troubling. Something was bothering him, she thought. "You looked like you were a thousand miles away."

"Only a thousand?" he teased. "I allotted you a million."

She lifted a shoulder casually, then let it drop again. "I'm not given to exaggeration."

He raised his brow, pretending to take offense. "Oh, and I am?"

"If the shoe fits." Before he could say anything in protest, she kissed him soundly, laughing halfway through it.

He could feel the joy spreading through him. Joy that being with her created. Sin-Jin gathered her closer to him.

"I was just thinking about the christening. What is it I'm supposed to do?"

"Nothing too taxing." Her eyes glinted with humor. They'd been through this before. Where was his famous memory now? "Just hold him during the ceremony and try not to drop him in the baptismal font."

"I'll do my best."

She leaned back and studied his face. "I don't know. I think I'd better test those arms of yours out, to see if they're strong enough. Purely for the purpose of research, of course."

''Of course.'' He tightened his arms around her. ''Strong enough?''

''Tighter.''

The humor faded a little as she hoped that somehow, if he held her close enough, tight enough, everything would eventually resolve itself. Like a fairy tale that came with a happily-ever-after guarantee.

''Tighter.''

He held her closer still, rocking with her in silence. Wanting to ask her what was wrong, but instinctively afraid of the answer.

Chapter Fifteen

Two mornings later Sherry stood watching as the priest poured holy water over her son's head and said words that linked one generation to another in a timeless ceremony. Her heart swelled as she watched Sin-Jin hold her son in his arms, a tender expression on his face.

It was in that moment that she knew.

It was gone.

Her resistance to ever becoming involved with another man, to ever loving another man, was gone.

Sherry knew that she was setting herself up to be hurt, that this relationship with Sin-Jin could not possibly be permanent. It was an interlude, nothing more. But that didn't change the fact that she wanted it to be permanent, wanted this man to be part of her life and she part of his.

But there was too much against it. Too many secrets between them.

Should she tell Sin-Jin of her discovery? Should she try to prod him for an explanation about his past, or pray that he suddenly wanted to tell her on his own? And now that they'd become intimate, why hadn't he told her on his own? Was he just passing the time with her? Was she just a filler until his interest waned?

And yet he was here and he didn't have to be. For all her pushiness, the man did not have to be here, taking on the mantle of godfather before a church full of people. That was of his own choosing.

There was no point in driving herself crazy with this, it wouldn't change anything.

And at least, she thought, smiling at Sin-Jin as he looked in her direction, she had the moment. That was all that life really was, perfect little moments strung together on a necklace of time.

She wanted more.

After the ceremony was over, she managed to herd everyone out of the small parking lot to the reception, which was being held at a restaurant belonging to one of her father's friends. Even Father Conway came along. The aging priest made a special point of singling Sin-Jin out and engaging him in lengthy conversations about the condition of business in the modern world. Sherry had her suspicions that her father had put the old priest up to it, but Sin-Jin didn't seem to mind sharing the car and his opinions, so she made no attempt to rescue him.

The party in the festively decorated banquet room continued until six o'clock, at which time a select few adjourned to Sherry's house for coffee and even more conversation.

Around eight, Father Conway said his goodbyes.

"I like your young man," he told her, his thick Irish brogue molding each syllable.

"He's not my young man," she'd protested. The last thing in the world she wanted was for the priest to get the wrong idea.

The priest looked genuinely disappointed. "That's a shame, because he's generous to a fault. Gave me a donation for the church right after the ceremony." He took out the check he'd slipped into his pocket and looked at it as if to assure himself that it was real. "This'll cover the rest of the new roof." And then he winked at her. "The Lord does move in mysterious ways." Beaming, he waved goodbye to Sin-Jin before taking his leave.

She sighed, closing the door. "That He does, Father, that He does."

It was ten o'clock before the last of her family and friends bade Sherry good-night and slipped out the door.

Exhausted, she blew out a breath. The first thing she did as soon as she closed the door was slip out of her shoes. She heard Sin-Jin laughing behind her.

Sherry turned around, looking at him quizzically. "What?"

"You always do that as soon as you're alone." Funny how he'd taken to noticing things about her. Without meaning to, the woman had managed to impress her actions on his brain.

It was suddenly very quiet in the room. She wondered if he planned to stay the night. Excitement began to slowly bubble through her. "But I'm not alone, you're here."

Yes, Sin-Jin thought, he was and he still wondered at it. Wondered how strange life sometimes was. Long ago he'd set aside the idea of ever having a family and yet here he was, being absorbed into hers and willingly so.

He slipped his arm around her shoulders. "Tired?" He kissed her temple.

All sorts of wonderful feelings began to take root within her. She wrapped her arms around him for a moment and nodded.

It had been a long day for her. "I can go," he offered.

"No." She placed a hand to his chest as he started to reach for his jacket. A warm, comfortable feeling spread out from beneath her hand. "Not yet," she whispered. Leaning her head back, she brushed a kiss against his lips. Her eyes met his in an unspoken promise of the night ahead. "Let me just go and check on Johnny."

He nodded, stepping back, getting out of her way.

Sherry rushed up the stairs.

The baby was sleeping peacefully. She lightly tucked his blanket around him, then kissed the tips of her fingers and just barely passed them along his cheek.

She had a baby she adored, a family who cared about her and a man she was falling in love with waiting downstairs. No matter what was waiting for her on the horizon, tonight she considered herself to be the luckiest woman on the face of the earth.

Walking out of the baby's room, Sherry stifled a

squeal as she felt her waist caught up from behind. Sin-Jin spun her around, and before she could say anything he had her against the wall, sealing his mouth to hers. Blotting out her words, her thoughts, the very world around her.

Nothing existed but him and the fire that was instantly ignited in her belly.

The kiss, powerful and demanding, drained her and somehow energized her at the same time. She didn't bother questioning it, she just went with the feeling.

Sherry wrapped her arms around his neck, pressing her eager body against the hard contours of his. He kissed her over and over again, raising her up off the floor. She wrapped her legs around his torso, demands running rampant through her, throbbing wildly.

She wanted him, wanted him badly. And he wanted her. She felt her blood sing as it pumped madly through her veins.

And then they were in her room, clothing flying everywhere, inert casualties to their mutual desires. Her body was on fire. And only Sin-Jin could put it out. But with each pass of his hands, each kiss pressed along her skin, the flames only rose higher.

He'd been downstairs waiting for her, debating whether or not he should just quietly withdraw and go home. He was in over his head and he knew it, was growing unnerved by it. She was changing him, taking him in directions he didn't want to go.

He'd made it all the way to the front door and then he'd thought of today, of being in the church and holding that small life in his arms, a life he'd helped bring into the world. He'd thought of the woman who had become such a huge part of his world in such an incredibly short amount of time, and suddenly desire had risen up and seized him by the throat, making it impossible for him to leave. Making even a minute longer without her incredibly hard to endure.

Acting on impulse, he'd raced up the stairs to be with her.

He knew he should go slower, savor the moment. He didn't want to frighten her. But the feelings that were ricocheting through his soul frightened him. *Frighten* was too genteel a word. They downright scared the hell right out of him.

The last time he'd been vulnerable was when he was a very young boy, watching his father leave home, a curvaceous woman on his arm who wasn't his mother. He remembered feeling lost and alone. Abandoned. To be vulnerable, to lay yourself bare to feelings, meant not being in control, not being able to save himself.

He'd vowed then never to be vulnerable again. Yet here he was, being vulnerable. Placing his soul into the small palm of a woman whose motives were not entirely certain.

It was insane, and yet, he just couldn't help himself. The ache in his belly, in his loins, in his heart, wouldn't let him help himself. He wanted her, this moment, here and now, he wanted her.

Pressing Sherry down against the bed, he held her captive as his lips raced along her body, anointing her flesh with hot, moist kisses that had her panting and twisting beneath him. With every movement she made, she excited him more, captivating him until he was utterly and completely her prisoner.

Unable to hold back any longer, Sin-Jin drove himself into her.

Her muffled cry of ecstasy against his lips began as the heated rhythm fused their hips together. Like a man possessed, he went faster and faster. Her arms wrapped around him, she kept pace.

When the final moment came, he felt as if an explosion had racked his body and yet, it wasn't enough.

He wanted more.

Exhausted, spent, he wanted more.

Was he completely crazy?

Dragging air into his lungs, Sin-Jin slid off her. He barely had enough energy to gather her body to him. Contentment blanketed him but didn't quite manage to cover his concerns.

Her heart was beating so hard Sherry was sure it was going to leap right out of her chest at any second. No matter, this was the best way to go, being made love to by a man she loved.

Passing a hand over her eyes, as if to help them focus, she could only lie there for a moment, doing her best to regulate her breathing. When she could finally manage to form words, she turned her face toward him. "Wow, what was that?"

He laughed shortly. It momentarily depleted his growing energy supply. "I'm not sure."

She smiled to herself. It was nice to know that he was as affected as she was. "Does the government know you have this secret weapon?"

He dragged another breath into his lungs. What

was it that she did to him? How was it that making love with her turned into an Olympic event? "I didn't even know I had it."

Gathering as much strength as she could, she rose up on one elbow and propped her head up, looking at him. Who would have ever thunk it? Sin-Jin Adair in her bed.

"If you ever tire of being a captain of industry, I promise you that you can make an incredible living as a gigolo." She spread her hand out, forming a horizon. "Women will be lining up for miles for just a sample of that."

He arched a brow. "I won't want women lining up for miles."

Her expression was the epitome of innocence. "Oh?"

He wanted to say that all he wanted was her, but that would place him at her mercy, and he couldn't allow that to happen, couldn't make himself that vulnerable.

The moment begged for something, for a revelation of some kind.

In a moment of weakness, when most of his guard was down, he told her, "That was my father's way." Tucking one hand under his head against his pillow, Sin-Jin pulled her closer with the other. He stared at the ceiling. "And my mother's."

Her heart began to hammer hard again. It took effort for her to make light of the moment, hoping that it would somehow encourage him to say more. Not because of any article she needed to write, but because she wanted him to trust her. "Your mother liked to have women line up for her?"

"No," he laughed, kissing the top of her head. And then the laughter died away as he remembered things he didn't want to. "They both liked to play change partners, though. A lot." She was quiet. Sin-Jin found her reaction unusual. And because she didn't ask, he heard himself telling her things he never meant to say. "My father was married five times before I lost count and interest. My mother, three." And he had disliked every one of the various spouses, because none of them had any use for him, making him feel more and more of an outsider in his own life.

He tried to sound philosophical. "I imagine by now I'd have to hire a stadium to properly celebrate Mother's Day and Father's Day in order to accommodate all the stepmothers and stepfathers I've acquired." His mouth curved cynically. "Not that any of them would come if invited."

They had shut him out, she thought. Sherry raised herself up again and looked down at him. "Oh, Sin-Jin, I'm so sorry."

He shrugged the sentiment away. "Don't be. Being a distant fifth wheel made me strong. It made me determined to be my own person, to never rely on anyone else for my happiness."

Was he putting her on notice? Telling her that this was nice, but don't get used to it? Now wasn't the time to think of her own feelings, she warned herself. He was sharing something, something hurtful from a past he'd kept locked away. This was about him, not her.

"That shouldn't have been a decision made by a young boy." She truly ached for him. Sherry caressed his face, wishing she could have made things different for him. No wonder he felt the way he did. "Every child should have a warm, loving family."

He blew out a dismissive breath. "Yes, well, there seems to be a slight shortage of those. At least where I was. I decided that that kind of thing was highly overrated."

She knew that was the act of a child attempting to protect himself. And the child was the father of the man. Right at this moment she hated the emotionally crippled couple that had given birth to him.

"Money being the only stable factor in my life, I decided to make some of my own. So as soon as I was able," he told her, "I took the money that my grandfather had left me in his will, left the place that was supposedly my home and went to college." He didn't bother saying which one, but that was a matter of record. He closed his eyes, remembering how hard it had been for him. "Along the way I shed my name and my family. I don't think either one of the two principal players even noticed. They were too busy with their own lives."

He opened his eyes, staring straight ahead. He couldn't remember what his parents looked like anymore. If he passed them on the street, would he know? Or would he just keep walking?

"They always had been. Which was all right," he said a second later, "because I was busy forging mine. Making connections and reinventing myself."

When Sherry reached for him, he pushed her hand aside, stiffening. He shouldn't have said anything. What had gotten into him? "I don't want your pity."

He was shutting her out. Just like his parents had

shut him out. Putting her own pain aside, she looked at him incredulously.

"Why would I pity a man who went on to become a force to be reckoned with? Who didn't wallow in self-pity but made something of himself? If anything, what I'm feeling right now is sympathy for the small boy who shouldn't have had to grow up in a house with no love. Who left home and felt that no one cared."

When he turned his face away, she physically forced his face back to make him look at her.

"Sympathy," she emphasized, "not pity. Pity is for the person who lets life knock him down and refuses to get up again. There is nothing pitiful about you, Sin-Jin. There never has been."

But there was, he thought. It was pitiful to him that he felt so lost without her, that his body was spent and all he could think of was making love with her again. Not because he had any physical needs. That would have been easier to accept. Men had needs. But he couldn't lie to himself. He wanted to make love with her because he needed and wanted this woman.

Needed and wanted Sherry.

And to need was to be vulnerable. And to be vulnerable was to be pitied.

His mouth curved slightly. "You do know how to stroke a man's ego."

"That wasn't stroking, that was the truth." And then she smiled up into his eyes. "But if you want to see stroking," she told him mischievously, slipping her hand down beneath the tangled sheet, finding him. "I can show you stroking."

Her fingertips lightly closed over him, her thumb passing over the tip of his shaft. Her hand just barely made contact as she moved her palm tantalizingly up and then down, over and over again. She felt him grow from wanting her. Her smile deepened.

"You know just how to get to me, don't you?" he breathed. Within a moment he had shifted so that he was over her again.

"Do I?" she wanted to know. Her smile faded as desire took root again. *Want me, Sin-Jin. Love me.* "Do I really?"

He pretended to breathe a sigh of relief. "Thank God, the questions are back." He laughed, and his breath tingled the skin along her throat, making the very core of her tighten in anticipation. "I was becoming worried. You didn't ask me any questions while I was telling you about my parents."

Guilt chewed at the fabric of the illusion she was trying to maintain for just a little while longer. Just for tonight. Tomorrow she would tell him the truth, that she already knew everything that he'd told her. Tomorrow, not tonight.

For tonight she sought refuge in half truths, praying she'd be forgiven. "You were telling me what you wanted me to know."

"Was I?" He kissed each of her breasts in turn, fascinated at the way her breathing became more labored. "Or were you just pulling it out of me like the sorceress that you are?"

"Is that what you think I am, a sorceress?" She rather liked the description. One of her favorite characters in literature was Morgana Le Fey, King Arthur's half sister. Seen as evil by some, she was still a fascinating character.

''Come to your own conclusion.'' He paused, knitting a wreath of openmouthed kisses over her quivering abdomen. ''You certainly cast a spell over me. I've just said things to you, told you things I haven't said to anyone else.'' She moaned as he licked her belly. A recklessness came over him. He slid his body along hers until he was looking into her eyes. ''Did you know that my name is really John Fletcher?''

She didn't want to lie, but telling him the truth now would ruin everything. Would steal him away from her. She knew it.

So instead of answering, she threaded her arms around his neck and brought him down to her abruptly, seizing his lips and kissing him as hard as she could. Praying that the question would slip his mind.

The question he'd just uttered vanished in a haze of desire. He'd already talked too much. It was time to stop talking and to make love with her.

Sin-Jin gathered her into his arms and gave himself up to the demands of his body and hers.

The soft, crying sound coming from the monitor on the nightstand had her opening her eyes immediately.

The baby was hungry, she thought, sitting up groggily. She looked at the clock beside the monitor. Almost four. Just like clockwork, she thought, smiling to herself. It gave Johnny something in common with his godfather.

Last night and the wee hours of this morning came back to her in brilliant hues. They'd made love three times, each time more frantic than the last. It was as if Sin-Jin couldn't get enough of her. That made it mutual.

As her feet touched the floor, she turned to see if the baby had woken Sin-Jin.

Her heart froze.

His side of the bed was empty.

She stretched her hand out to touch where he'd slept. The sheet was cold.

And his clothes were gone.

Chapter Sixteen

Maybe Johnny had cried earlier and she just hadn't heard him. Maybe Sin-Jin had gotten up to look in on the boy and hadn't wanted to wake her up.

Mentally crossing her fingers, Sherry hurried into her son's room.

Sin-Jin wasn't in the nursery.

Johnny was awake, fussing in his crib, trying to shove his fist into his mouth. Cooing softly to soothe him, she picked the infant up.

Slipping her hand beneath his bottom at least told her what part of the problem was. "You're wet, huh? Well, we can fix that. Just hang on a second longer, okay?"

Sin-Jin had to be in the house; he couldn't have just left without saying a word.

Could he?

With the baby tucked into the crook of her arm, Sherry went out into the hall again and crossed to the head of the stairs, hoping that perhaps he'd gone to the kitchen to make a pot of coffee.

Sin-Jin was just opening the front door, on his way out.

"Wait."

He stopped dead and looked up toward the top of the stairs. It was evident by the look on his face that he'd hoped to be out of the house by the time she woke up.

Damn it, why?

It wasn't a time for banter, but it was the only way for her to hide the suddenly panicky feeling that was clawing its way up within her. She would have come down the stairs if she could have, but her knees felt frozen in place.

He was leaving. Permanently. Think. Say something to keep him from going.

"You don't have to sneak out, you know." Sherry forced a smile to her lips. "I won't make you change his diaper."

He was behaving like a coward and he hated it. But he'd wanted to be gone before she woke up. Before she looked at him with those eyes of hers, those eyes that made him forget everything else except her.

Before he wanted to make love with her again.

It was too late for that. He could feel the stirrings beginning already. He slammed them down. The consequences of following his impulses were too costly. They were already costing him. Dearly. He'd seen that last night. Time to get out before he couldn't.

Damn, why couldn't she have slept just a little longer?

Uncomfortable, he cleared his throat. "Look, this was a mistake."

Stunned, feeling like a single-engine plane caught in a tailspin, Sherry could only stare at him. She'd never felt more isolated in her life. There were suddenly a million miles between them.

Maybe she hadn't heard right. Maybe she was stuck in some kind of time warp.

"What?" she whispered hoarsely.

"This went a little too far," he told her. A helplessness was drenching him. The frustration he felt angered Sin-Jin. "It was nice, but—"

She held her baby against her. Her eyes widened as she continued staring at him incredulously. "Nice? You call these last weeks 'nice'?"

It was a bland word, meant to be applied to a cut of clothing, not to what was happening between them.

But maybe nothing *was* happening between them, maybe it was all in her head, all one-sided. Could she be that blind not to realize?

No, it wasn't possible.

Was it?

"Yes, nice," he repeated with emphasis, wanting to be anywhere but here, anyone but him. "But I think it's over. I said some things last night..."

He stopped, not knowing how to end the sentence, knowing only that he felt threatened. And he hated to feel threatened. What the hell had he been thinking of, saying those things to her? Baring his soul to a woman he knew was a reporter? For all he knew, she might have been playing him all along.

His eyes darkened. "If I see a word of what I told you in print, your paper'll face a lawsuit the magnitude of which you can't even begin to imagine. By the time my lawyers are finished with the *Bedford World News,* it will be completely bankrupt." The words were coming out of his mouth, but it felt as if someone else was saying them. Still, he couldn't stop them. "I won't have my privacy invaded."

Numb, she felt as if someone had just ripped out her heart and left a gaping hole in its place. "Your privacy?" she echoed. "This is about your privacy?"

She wanted to scream at Sin-Jin, to beat on him with both fists until he took it back, until he came to his senses. But there was a baby in her arms and he came first, before her own feelings. Johnny was growing progressively fussier, as if he was reacting to the agitation going on inside of her. She couldn't even raise her voice. But her eyes said it all.

"Well, the hell with your privacy, John Fletcher, or St. John Adair, or whatever you want to call yourself. And the hell with you."

With that, she turned her back on him and walked back to the nursery.

He wanted to rush up after her, to sweep her into his arms and apologize. But it was better this way. Better for her, better for him.

Sin-Jin slammed the door as he left.

As she laid Johnny in his crib, the sound vibrated

within her chest. Sherry caught her lower lip between her teeth to keep from crying.

He waited for the story to appear in the paper. For ten days he waited. Each day that it didn't, he grew progressively more restless, progressively more uncertain of his actions. Had he been wrong to end it?

No.

Yes.

He didn't know.

Sin-Jin threw himself into work, arriving early, staying late. His temper shortened, his disposition deteriorated, and his fuse became nonexistent. He caught himself snapping at everyone and regretting it, but lacking the ability to right the situation.

He was a man in hell.

And then, after what seemed like the umpteenth sleepless night, he came to terms with his demons and began setting his house in order. The first order of business was to call Sherry and humbly apologize.

She wasn't home.

He kept calling, getting her answering machine and growing progressively more and more irritable.

Ten calls later he was sitting at his desk at work, debating whether or not he should go over to her house in person and set siege to her door. He'd taken over entire corporations with less difficulty than he was having trying to find this woman.

Another futile attempt had him slamming down his phone receiver. Where the hell *was* she?

He heard the slight tap on his door and knew better than to hope that Sherry would be standing on the other side. He did, anyway.

"Come in."

Mrs. Farley walked quietly in and placed a single printed sheet on his desk, then took a step back.

Disappointed, Sin-Jin frowned at the paper without picking it up. He didn't recall asking for anything. "What's this?"

Mrs. Farley laced her hands together primly. "I believe if you read it, you'll see that it's a letter of resignation."

He felt as if a bomb had just been detonated beneath his feet. "Yours?"

She inclined her head. "Mine. Although," she said, "it will probably be the first of many."

Picking it up, he scanned the sheet without really seeing it. This had to be some kind of mistake. Mrs. Farley was the most steadfast part of his life. "I don't understand."

"Neither do we, John." If the letter hadn't gotten his full attention, her addressing him by his real first name would have. Mrs. Farley rarely ever called him that. When she did, it was because she was deadly serious and meant business. "Ever since last Monday, you've become this surly, unapproachable man whose only order of business seems to be biting people's heads off."

He'd been like a man who could not find a place for himself within his own skin. It had taken him almost two weeks of grappling with his soul, with the past that he'd wanted to keep buried, to come to the conclusion that he had allowed ghosts to rob him of his only happiness. The specter of his parents' failed liaisons had egged him on to sabotage his one true chance at happiness.

He realized that what he had failed to take into the equation, on that morning he'd run for his life, were the personalities of his parents and of the people they chose to have their relationships with. Not a one of them was equal to Sherry.

And he was not his parents. For as long as he could remember, they had been comfortable coasting through life, never contributing, never attempting to leave a mark or make the world even a minutely better place than they had found it. That wasn't him. The contributions he made to various charities attested to that. Since he couldn't care for one person, he'd cared for many.

But now it was time to take the training wheels off. To care for the one. Because she had finally come into his life.

Looking at the letter of resignation, he knew he'd already made up his mind to go to Sherry and get on his knees if he had to, to get her to forgive him his temporary foray into the land of the insane.

But first there was a fire to put out. He raised his eyes to the thin, regal-looking woman standing by his desk. "I'm sorry, Mrs. Farley."

She sighed delicately. "And so am I. You're a good man, John." Her eyes narrowed behind her glasses. "Whatever's wrong in your life, fix it."

That was exactly what he intended to do. Sin-Jin smiled at her as he crumpled up the letter of resignation. "Absolutely." He held up the ball of paper. "May I throw this out?"

She paused. Married at twenty-three, childless and widowed at thirty, she had always regarded the man at the desk as the son she would have loved to have had.

"If you promise to stop this nonsense and go back to being the man I've always been proud of, yes, you may throw it out."

"It's a deal." He pitched the wadded-up resignation into his wastepaper basket. As he reached for the telephone to try one last time to get through to Sherry before he went to her physically, it rang beneath his hand.

Ever the guardian, Mrs. Farley moved his hand aside and picked up the receiver. "Adair Industries, Mr. Adair's office." She paused, listening, then placed the call on hold. "Are you in for a Rusty Thomas? He says he's a friend of Ms. Campbell's and that this is urgent."

Something suddenly tightened in his gut, stealing his breath away. Sin-Jin extended his hand for the receiver. "Give it to me. I'll take it."

He barely had time to say hello before the man on the other end began talking.

"Look, Mr. Adair, I'm a friend of Sherry's," Rusty told him. "She'd kill me if she knew I was calling, but her son's in the hospital."

Sin-Jin was on his feet instantly. "What hospital, where? Why?"

For once in his life, Rusty had very little information and it confounded him. "Blair Memorial. There's something wrong with his heart and—"

Sin-Jin hung up. His face was ashen as he looked at Mrs. Farley. "Have my car waiting by the time I get to the lobby," he requested, hurrying out the door. "And tell Carver to take over."

He's back, Mrs. Farley thought, dialing. She crossed her fingers that everything was all right.

Sin-Jin didn't remember driving. He remembered getting into his car and then arriving at Blair. The way to the hospital was a blur of twists and turns and yellow lights he just barely squeaked through.

There was something wrong with the baby and she hadn't called him.

Damn it, didn't she know he'd be there for her? For the baby?

How the hell could she? he upbraided himself. The last thing he'd done was threaten her with a lawsuit. You didn't turn to people like that in your time of need. You did your best to avoid them. He knew that.

He cursed himself savagely.

Not bothering to search through the lot for a space, Sin-Jin surrendered his Mercedes to the parking valet at the hospital's entrance. Tossing the keys toward the attendant, he raced through the electronic doors.

He'd barely made it inside when he heard the valet calling after him. "Hey, mister. Mister! You forgot your ticket."

The attendant ran after him. Sin-Jin paused only long enough to grab the ticket that the red-vested man thrust at him. "Thanks." The valet looked a little wary of him as he stepped back.

Sin-Jin caught sight of his reflection in the glass doors. He looked like a madman. He did his best to pull himself together. Frightening hospital personnel wouldn't help him find Sherry and the baby.

The information desk was immediately to his left. "I'm looking for a Sherry Campbell," he told the woman behind the desk. "No, wait, I mean John Campbell. He would have been admitted sometime today, yesterday, I'm not sure," he confessed.

"What for?" the woman asked kindly.

"He's an infant," Sin-Jin began, realizing that his thoughts were scattered like so many raindrops in a storm. "Heart trouble," he clarified. "I'm sorry, I really don't—"

"Right here," the woman informed him softly, her finger isolating the baby's name on her screen. "He's in the neonatal section. Admitted last night."

Last night. While he had been calling her. Guilt twisted inside of him.

"That's on the—"

"I know where it is," he said, cutting her off, then adding, "Thank you," before he turned on his heel.

As he began to hurry down the corridor that eventually led to the tower elevators, something made him look toward his right, toward the small, serene room that served as the hospital's chapel.

She was there.

His heart stood still. Walking to the entrance of the small room on someone else's feet, he called out to her, his voice throbbing with emotion.

"Sherry."

At first she thought she only imagined his voice. Kneeling, her head bowed, Sherry had been praying so hard that she'd lost track of her surroundings and the time. She'd left her parents upstairs with the baby and had come down here to ask for help.

Almost afraid, she turned away from the cross on the wall. He was standing in the entrance.

Sin-Jin.

He looked like an answer to a prayer.

She rose to her feet in slow motion. Her first impulse was to throw herself into his arms, to sob her heart out and somehow have him take the pain away.

But she'd been so hurt, felt so abandoned when he'd left, she couldn't bring herself to risk being rebuffed again. When Drew had walked out on her, she'd been devastated, but that feeling didn't begin to compare with the way she'd felt when Sin-Jin had left her that morning. Like there was no reason to go on.

But there was a reason, there was Johnny. She needed to go on, to be strong for him. And now her baby was ill. She didn't know if she could bear it.

"What are you doing here?"

Her voice was cold, distant. He knew he deserved it, but it still hurt to hear her like that. Hurt to think that she was going through this without him. "More important, what are you doing here without me?"

Feeling lost. She tossed her head, trying hard to look strong, to look as if what he had done to her hadn't gutted the very foundations of her world. "Doing the very best I can."

He made his way into the room slowly, invading her space an inch at a time. "Why didn't you call me?"

How could he even ask her that question? "Why?" she echoed incredulously. "Because you made it perfectly clear that you didn't want me in your life."

"I was an ass."

The bluntness of his admission took the wind out

of her sails. Her hastily newly reconstructed defenses slipped. ''Nobody's arguing.''

''Look.'' Taking her hand, Sin-Jin sat down with her in the pew. ''It doesn't really justify anything, but there's a lot of baggage in my life, a lot of emotional scarring. I was afraid to get involved, afraid to allow myself to love someone because I didn't want to get on that merry-go-round that my parents were on.'' He looked into her eyes, praying she could understand. ''Didn't want to have my heart ripped out of me.''

She shook her head. She understood in theory, but not in practice. How could he think that of her? ''Did I look like the kind of person who goes around ripping people's hearts out for a hobby?''

He couldn't help smiling at the ludicrousness of the image. ''No.''

Sherry threw up her hands helplessly. ''Well then?''

He could only resort to the simple phrase, meaning it from the bottom of his heart. ''I'm sorry.''

Her world had been tipped over in the past twenty-four hours, ever since she'd taken Johnny in to his pediatrician, her mother's instinct telling her that something was wrong with her baby. He'd been too listless lately.

She hated being right.

Sherry shrugged, looking away. ''Doesn't matter, anyway.''

Sin-Jin took hold of her hand, forcing her to look at him.

''Yes, it does,'' he insisted. ''It matters a great deal. It matters to me. For what it's worth, Sherry, I love you and I want to take care of you.'' He'd never meant anything more in his life. ''You and Johnny.''

She drew herself up, unconsciously still leaving her hands in his. ''I don't need anyone to take care of me.'' Didn't he understand? ''I need someone to be there, that's all.''

He intended to do whatever it took. ''Then I'll be there,'' he swore. ''And I'll help take care of Johnny.''

Emotions warred within her. She was afraid to believe him. Afraid and, oh, so tired. She felt as if the past twenty-four hours had been an eternity. ''Don't put yourself out.''

''I'm not, damn it. I want to.'' He struggled to contain his temper. ''I will do whatever it takes to make you forgive me.'' He was pleading now, fighting for his very life. She had to forgive him. ''You want me in a hair shirt, you got it. You want it in skywriting, you got it.'' His voice became deadly serious. ''You want to publish that article, you got it. I'll even give you details. It'll be your exclusive.''

The article didn't matter. It'd stopped mattering the night of her son's christening, when he had let her into his life, however briefly. She knew she couldn't betray that trust, no matter the professional cost.

She shook her head. ''All I want is for my son to be all right.''

He felt his heart twisting in his chest, wishing he could take the burden off her shoulders. ''What's wrong with him?''

There was a long, technical name for the condition. Dr. DuCane had been very patient, very kind as she had explained it to her. She'd called in a heart surgeon, a Dr. Lukas Graywolf, and between the two of them, they had gone over everything with her and her parents. It had all boiled down to one thing for her: Johnny's heart had a slight tear and needed to be operated on. If it wasn't, he might not make it to his fifth birthday.

"He needs corrective heart surgery. He's in surgery right now." She looked up at him. "And I am so scared."

He took her into his arms. "So am I." She looked at him, stunned by the admission. "But he'll be all right. I swear to you he'll be all right. He'll have the finest doctors in the world. Whatever it takes. And when he gets through this—and he will—he can be our ring bearer."

"Ring bearer?" Her mind felt like a vast wasteland. She tried to focus and make sense of what he was saying to her. "He's only two months old."

He had that covered. "Mrs. Farley can push him in a carriage. We'll run a string through the ring and attach it to his hand. Greta will even trot at his side. It'll work."

She stared at him, dumbfounded. "Are you—are you proposing to me?"

He knew he was making a mess of it, but this wasn't an area he had any experience in. "Badly—but this is my first time. My only time," he amended. "Unless you say no, then I plan to ask you every day of your life until you say yes."

And suddenly she knew. It was going to be all right. Everything was going to be all right. She smiled at him. "I guess it would save us a lot of time if I said yes, then."

He breathed a sigh of relief. "Definitely more efficient."

She pressed her lips together, suppressing a giddy laugh. "You're an idiot, you know that?"

Twice in one day. "Mrs. Farley already beat you to that description. Not in so many words, but the general gist was there."

She allowed herself a moment longer in his arms. "Why, did you ask her to marry you, too?"

"No, only you." He rose from the pew. "I know that I probably don't deserve you two, but I want the three of us to be a family. You, me and that wonderful son of yours. I want him to be my son, too." A part of him thought that he probably had all along.

"I guess, since you were the first one to hold him, it's only fair."

"That's all I want, my fair share of you." He kissed her and she clung to him. It took them both a moment to realize that they weren't alone.

Sherry's eyes widened with fear as she looked at her son's heart surgeon. "Is he—" She couldn't bring herself to finish the sentence. Her heart wouldn't let her.

Tall, stately Lukas Graywolf was quick to set her at ease. "Your son pulled through with flying colors. He's going to be fine." He smiled. "Your mother told me where to find you. Whatever you two said in here—" he nodded toward the altar "—obviously worked. He's in recovery right now, but you'll be able to see him when they bring him back to the intensive care unit—just a precaution,'' he explained when he saw the look on her face. ''I'll be by later.''

She clasped his hand. ''Thank you, Doctor.''

''Just doing my job.'' He hurried away.

Sherry took the handkerchief Sin-Jin held out and dried her eyes. ''I guess you brought us luck.''

He took her into his arms again. ''That goes double for me.''

As he kissed her, Sin-Jin knew he wasn't alone anymore.

Epilogue

"My God, Sheila, there's enough food here to feed the city of San Francisco." Walking into the kitchen, Connor Campbell shook his head at the wealth of plates spread out on the kitchen table. His wife had added two extra leaves to it just to accommodate all the various items.

Sheila continued arranging the various trays. "Better too much than too little. We don't want to run out on your grandson's first birthday party, do you?"

Connor came up behind his wife and wrapped his arms around her waist, hugging her to him. "So, you're finally okay with 'Grandma'?"

"As long as it's Johnny who's calling me that, yes. But don't you be getting no ideas that you'll be referring to me that way." She turned around to face her husband, a look of warning in her eye. "Or you'll find yourself sleeping on the couch, Connor Francis Campbell.''

''Uh-uh.'' Sin-Jin walked in to join them. ''Three names, sounds like she means it, Connor,'' he teased.

Connor locked his arms around Sheila again. ''Go tend to your own wife,'' he said to his son-in-law. ''I'll handle mine.''

Sin-Jin was the soul of innocence. He indicated the empty bowl he was carrying. ''Just came in to refill the pasta salad bowl. They're eating as if they've been starved for three days.''

Sheila was looking at her husband, her hands on her hips as she wrestled out of his hold. '''Handle' now is it?''

Connor raised his hands in abject surrender. ''Just an expression, love, just an expression.''

Sin-Jin laughed as, bowl refilled, he made his exit from his in-laws' kitchen to the living room.

Sherry saw him laughing as she approached. ''What's going on in there?'' She nodded toward the kitchen.

''Just your parents clearing up some semantics.'' Putting the bowl down on the buffet table, he looked at the crowded room. Between Sherry's friends, the people his in-laws had invited and the selected few he'd asked from his office, there was hardly any space to move about. His son, the guest of honor, was in the middle of a group of loving admirers. He'd recovered with remarkable speed from his surgery and was the picture of health. Mrs. Farley was holding him, beaming. It was a nice look for her, Sin-Jin thought.

He nuzzled Sherry. ''Think we have enough people?''

She laughed, loving the feel of his arms around her. It was something she knew she would never take for granted. Her son was healthy and happy, and Owen had just told her that he was promoting her to investigative reporter, even though the article on Sin-Jin had never materialized. Life just couldn't get any better. "We could always send out for more."

"Actually—" he brushed a kiss against her hair "—I was thinking of slipping away myself."

"Not before the cake," she warned. "Mom worked on it all day."

Sin-Jin smiled down at his wife. "I've already got my cake. And I'm thinking of nibbling on it, too." He kissed her ear.

"I'll hold you to that." Taking his wrist in her hand, she looked at his battered watch, marking the time. "At twenty-two hundred hours...bedroom."

He looked down at his watch. It was only four in the afternoon. An eternity away.

"You're on, Mrs. Adair."

Sin-Jin began counting down the minutes.

* * * * *

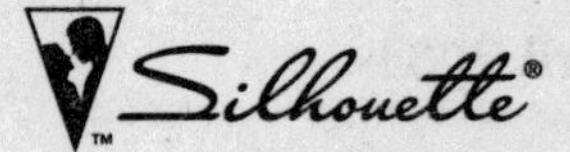

SPECIAL EDITION®

COMING NEXT MONTH

#1531 CONFLICT OF INTEREST—Gina Wilkins
The McClouds of Mississippi
Reclusive writer Gideon McCloud was definitely not baby-sitter material. So, when left to care for his half sister, he persuaded the beautiful Adrienne Corley to help. As his once-empty house filled with love and laughter, his heart began to yearn…for a family—and for Adrienne!

#1532 SHOWDOWN!—Laurie Paige
Seven Devils
Who was Hannah Carrington? Zack Dalton's cop instincts told him there was more to his supposedly long-lost relative than met the eye. Would discovering the gorgeous dancer wasn't who she seemed leave Zack feeling betrayed, or free to pursue the heady feelings she awakened in him?

#1533 THE TROUBLE WITH JOSH—Marilyn Pappano
Handsome rancher Josh Rawlins wanted forever. Blond beauty Candace Thompson couldn't even promise tomorrow. After a near-fatal bout with a serious illness, Candace was not looking for romance. But being with Josh made her feel like anything was possible. Could Josh and Candace find a way to take a chance on love?

#1534 THE MONA LUCY—Peggy Webb
Pretending to be in love with the charming Sandi Wentworth was not what commitment-phobic Matt Coltrane had planned to do. But that was exactly what he *had* to do to keep his ailing mother happy. The sparks that flew whenever Matt and Sandi were together were undeniable, and soon it began to feel less like pretend…and more like the real thing.…

#1535 EXPECTING THE CEO'S BABY—Karen Rose Smith
Widow Jenna Winton was shocked when she was told the lab had mixed her deceased husband's sperm sample with another man's. Then she met CEO Blake Winston, the father of her child, and the sizzling attraction between them was almost more than she could resist!

#1536 HIS PRETEND WIFE—Lisette Belisle
When an accident left loner Jake Slade unconscious with no one to speak for him, Abby Pierce stepped up to the task. Abby would do anything to help Jake—even if it meant pretending to be his wife. When Jake finally woke, he found he'd gained a blushing bride whose tender care was healing both his body…and his heart.

SSECNM0303